GUNSMOKE ON THE RIO GRANDE

GUNSMOKE ON THE RIO GRANDE

Bradford Scott

GUNSMOKE

First published in the US by Pyramid Books

This hardback edition 2012
by AudioGO Ltd
by arrangement with
Golden West Literary Agency

ISBN 978 1 445 85070 2

British Library Cataloguing in Publication Data available.

Printed and bound in Great Britain by the MPG Books Group

Bradford Scott was a pseudonym for **Leslie Scott** who was born in Lewisburg, West Virginia. During the Great War, he joined the French Foreign Legion and spent four years in the trenches. In the 1920s he worked as a mining engineer and bridge builder in the western American states and in China before settling in New York. A bar-room discussion in 1934 with Leo Margulies, who was managing editor for Standard Magazines, prompted Scott to try writing fiction. He went on to create two of the most notable series characters in Western pulp magazines. In 1936, Standard Magazines launched, and in *Texas Rangers*, Scott under the house name of **Jackson Cole** created Jim Hatfield, Texas Ranger, a character whose popularity was so great with readers that this magazine featuring his adventures lasted until 1958. When others eventually began contributing Jim Hatfield stories, Scott created another Texas Ranger hero, Walt Slade, better known as *El Halcon*, the Hawk, whose exploits were regularly featured in *Thrilling Western*. In the 1950s Scott moved quickly into writing book-length adventures about both Jim Hatfield and Walt Slade in long series of original paperback Westerns. At the same time, however, Scott was also doing some of his best work in hardcover Westerns published by Arcadia House; thoughtful, well-constructed stories, with engaging characters and authentic settings and situations. Among the best of these, surely, are *Silver City* (1953), *Longhorn Empire* (1954), *The Trail Builders* (1956), and *Blood on the Rio Grande* (1959). In these hardcover Westerns, many of which have never been reprinted, Scott proved himself highly capable of writing traditional Western stories with characters who have sufficient depth to change in the course of the narrative and with a degree of authenticity and historical accuracy absent from many of his series stories.

1

RANGER WALT SLADE, he whom the Mexican peons of the River villages named *El Halcon*—The Hawk—chuckled as he recalled the solemn and somewhat pompous verbiage of a contemporary historian anent the city of Laredo on the Rio Grande:

"Laredo maintains a fairly normal state of existence. Bandits from across the river, outlaws from the brush country, and organized bands of cattle thieves create some mild excitement. Pirates prey on the river traffic. The outlaws make the highways unsafe. Laredo receives, with equal frequency, the bullets and the refugees of battles between rival Mexican factions in Nuevo Laredo on the south bank of the river. Deserters from the various factions loot both sides of the river impartially, when able to do so. The number of sudden deaths from violent causes remains about stable."

And toward the "peaceful" city of Laredo on the Rio Grande, Ranger Walt Slade rode blithely.

"Well, Shadow," he told his tall black horse, "I've a notion we'll have a real nice time at that pueblo over by the river."

Shadow's snort was derisive. Slade chuckled and rode on.

The trail running through the brush country and flanked on either side by tall chaparral, was a twisting one. Directly ahead was a sharp bend, and suddenly from around the bend came a scream of pain, another and another. Slade straightened in the saddle.

"Get going, feller," he said sharply. "Something going on around that curve."

Shadow shot forward, flashed around the bend. Slade twitched the reins and he came to a sliding halt. Slade leaned forward, gazing with narrowed eyes.

Beside the trail stood four horses and a mule, and in a little clearing which cut into the brush stood four men. Roped to the trunk of a small tree was an old Mexican. There were bloody welts crisscrossing his naked back. One of the men, big and beefy with thick shoulders and long arms and a truculent face, was just raising a heavy quirt to strike again when Slade's voice thundered at him.

"Hold it! What the devil's going on here?"

The man turned, glaring angrily. "Listen, cowboy," he said in a rumbling growling voice, "we're of the Land Committee and we don't want any interference from range tramps. Get going!"

"Land Committee?" Slade said, his voice deceptively mild. "Seems to me that if you are a fair to middling specimen, Committee of Skunks would be more fitting."

The big man swelled like an enraged turkey cock; but before he could answer, the old Mexican twisted around to stare at Slade. A glad cry burst from his lips:

"*El Halcon!*"

The effect was magical. The four men seemed to shrivel as they stared wide-eyed at the legendary figure whose exploits, some of them apparently questionable, were talked about with awe, anger, and respect throughout Texas—"The singingest man in the whole Southwest, with the fastest gun hand."

The big man spoke, his voice suddenly high and reedy, "Are you *El Halcon?*"

"Been called that," Slade admitted. "But you haven't answered my question. What's going on here?"

The big man answered. "This saddle-colored hellion was told to get out," he said. "He didn't, so we're teaching him a little lesson in what it means to buck the committee."

"I see," Slade said quietly. "Taking the law in your own hands, eh? Not a very nice thing to do."

The big man had recovered some of his aplomb. "And if what I've heard of you is true, you're a nice one to say that," he sneered.

"What you've heard may or may not be true," Slade replied. Apparently his attention was fixed on the speaker. In fact, however, he was watching another man, a scrawny little rat-faced individual who stood apart from the others. His left hand moved, a blurred flicker like to the shearing wing of a speeding hawk. There was the crash of a shot.

The three men jumped with startled yelps. Rat-face fell to the ground, screaming his agony and clawing at his blood-spurting hand. The gun he had stealthily drawn, one buttplate shattered, lay yards distant.

Slade, his long-barreled Colt wisping smoke, flicked his attention to the other three. To the fourth he paid no further mind; Rat-face was too white and sick to do anything but writhe and moan. A forty-five slug through the hand is no light matter, especially when a gun handle hurls its flattened point back sideways through the mangled flesh. .

"Anybody else in the notion to start fanging?" Slade asked pleasantly. "If so, get going; only next time I shoot at a hand I'm liable to miss—about six inches *inside*."

The significance of the remark was not lost on his hearers. They glared and mouthed, but kept their hands still.

Slade holstered his gun with effortless ease. "All right," he said. "Fork your bronks and get going. Haul that sidewinder up and take him with you; he isn't killed. Move!"

The last word blared at them like steel grinding on ice; they moved. The big man turned slowly, his face working with rage. His companions, nondescript specimens of medium build and height, who, nevertheless, Slade would instantly recognize if he saw them again, jerked retching and gagging Rat-face to his feet and led him, reeling and lurching, to where the horses stood. The big man, with an oath, seized him by the collar and the seat of his overalls and fairly hurled him into the saddle. Then he turned to Slade.

"This isn't finished, blast you," he said thickly. "We'll be looking for you, and there's others who'll be looking for you, too."

"You may not enjoy finding me," Slade replied. "Get going. The trail runs straight for about a mile, I see," he added. "And this saddle gun of mine carries quite a way, so it might be a good notion not to turn off anywhere this side of the next bend."

His hand dropped to the butt of the heavy Winchester protruding from the saddle boot under his muscular left thigh as he spoke. The big man muttered another oath and mounted. His companions wasted no time in following his example. With the moaning Rat-face bringing up the rear, the quartet moved down the trail. Slade watched them dwindle into the distance. Then he dismounted and approached the old Mexican, who was sagging in his bonds. A few strokes with a knife freed him and Slade gently eased him to the ground.

"Stretch out on your face," he directed. "I have some salve in my saddle pouch that'll ease the smart. You all right otherwise?"

"*Si, Capitan*," the old man replied, employing the Mexican term of respect. "They did not hurt me before the whip."

His slender, steely fingers as gentle as a woman's, Slade ministered to the old man's lacerated back. The Mexican retrieved his shirt from where it had been cast on the ground and donned it. He gratefully accepted the cigarette Slade rolled and lighted and took several deep and gratifying drags. Slade watched him until his nerves had steadied.

"*Gracias*," the old man said. 'Now I feel the much better."

"And now suppose you tell me what this is all about?" Slade prompted. He already knew what it was all about, which was the reason he was heading for Laredo, but he wanted to hear the Mexican's version.

"By the way," he added before the other could speak, "what is your name, *amigo?*"

"Cardena," the Mexican replied. "Felipe Cardena. I was named for my grandfather."

"Just one more question," Slade said. "It seems to me you speak English somewhat differently than do most of your countrymen."

Cardena smiled. "It is not strange," he said. "I was born in Texas, and so was my father before me."

"I see," Slade commented thoughtfully. "Then you are a Texan, and an American citizen."

"It is so," Cardena replied. "English is really my language, although of course I speak Spanish, and sometimes my way of speaking is not that of the Texans who came here from the east."

Slade nodded. "And Texans whose fathers came from New England don't speak just the same as those descended from Kentuckians or Virginians," he remarked. "Now, as to what this business today was about."

Leaning comfortably against the tree, Slade listened to a tale of wrong. Of Texas-Mexicans deprived of their homesteads of years by fraud or, the validity of their titles questioned, harrassed by legal technicalities until they gave up the fight in weariness and disgust and moved elsewhere. Of others driven from their lands by threats and intimidation. Of humble peons beaten, whipped, even murdered for their scanty holdings. As he listened his eyes grew colder and the concentration furrow deepened between his black brows, a sure sign that *El Halcon* was doing some hard thinking.

"In despair-we wrote to Captain McNelty, whom all men trust, and asked for help," Felipe concluded. "So far we have not.heard from him. Not that it matters anymore, however, now that *El Halcon* is here."

"*Gracias,*" Slade replied. "Captain Jim never lets anybody down, and I'll try not to betray your confidence."

"*El Halcon*, the friend of the lowly, does not betray," Felipe said with conviction. "And when *El Halcon* comes, evil departs."

"And I guess we'd better depart, if we're to get you home before dark," Slade said. "By the way, do you know those men who whipped you?"

"The large one is named Cale Brandon, he speaks for the Land Committee," Felipe replied. "The others I do not know."

Slade nodded. Stooping, he picked up the blood-stained whip which lay where Brandon dropped it and slipped it into one of his saddle pouches.

"Might come in handy, can't tell," he remarked. For a moment he stood gazing down the trail, his eyes thoughtful. Without doubt, a systematic campaign to drive the landowners, principally of Mexican descent, from the valley. But why? Well, it was up to him to find out why.

"Fork your mule and let's go," he told Felipe. "How did they happen to grab you?" he added as they got under way.

"I was riding the trail to my home, the home where my father was born," Felipe explained. "They rode from the chaparral and seized me. Cale Brandon had warned me that unless I left my land I would suffer harm."

"And you refused to let them have the land?"

"That is so," the other answered. "*Si*, I refused to leave, and I did suffer harm."

"I see," Slade nodded. "You hang onto your land and don't be intimidated."

"As *El Halcon* orders, I will do," the old man replied.

"You will ride wtih me to my house, *Capitan?* Doubtless, you feel hunger."

"You're darn right I do," Slade smiled. "My stomach's beginning to think my throat's cut. Let's go!"

When they reached the distant bend, Slade became alert and watchful, although he did not really expect any trouble with the unsavory quartet. Bird or beast would very likely warn him of an attempted ambush. Also, recent rain had softened the trail somewhat and to *El Halcon's* keen eyes the marks of the four horses were plain, especially those left by Rat-face's mount, which was not being held to a steady course. He would note any turning off in plenty of time to take precautions.

After several miles of riding they topped a slope, passed through a notch and the wide and shallow valley of the Rio Grande lay before them. To the southeast a feathery smudge of smoke against the sky marked the site of Laredo.

On the lip of the opposite sag, Slade halted Shadow and sat gazing over the scene below, mellowed and softened by the rays of the low-lying sun. His face wore a perplexed expression as he studied the valley where many Texas-Mexicans had their homes. Why he wondered, was somebody so anxious to drive them from the valley? The land they occupied was not particularly good, either for grazing or planting. On the delta where Brownsville stands at the mouth of the Rio Grande, flood waters had for centuries deposited silt that grew fine crops. Here it was different. The river, running swiftly in its deeply scoured-out bed, seldom over-flowed and there was very little deposit on the semi-arid lands. The small farmers managed to eke out a living from the soil and raise some cattle and sheep. That was about all. Nothing, it would seem, to warrant such an organized effort attended by vicious lawlessness. Slade couldn't figure it; not yet, at least.

While Slade gazed at the valley below, Felipe Cardena gazed at him. What a splendid looking man he was! Very tall, more than six feet, his broad shoulders and deep chest tapered down to a slender, sinewy waist about which were double cartridge belts. From the carefully worked and oiled cut out holsters protruded the plain black butts of his heavy guns. His face, deeply bronzed, was lean and high-nosed and dominated by long gray eyes, cold, reckless eyes that nevertheless always seemed to have little devils of laughter dancing in their clear depths. His rather wide mouth, grin-quirked at the corners, relieved somewhat the sternness, almost fierceness of the hawk nose above and the powerful chin and jaw beneath. His pushed back "J.B." revealed thick black hair. He wore the homely, efficient garb of the rangeland—faded blue shirt and Levis, vivid neckerchief looped at the open throat of his shirt, well scuffed half-boots of softly tanned leather. His magnificent black horse was full eighteen hands high and showed every indication of speed, intelligence and endurance.

Riding down the long and gentle slope they reached the level ground, passing humble homes, each with its patch of cultivated ground, and an occasional more pretentious building. Cattle and sheep grazed on the grassland, but there were no great herds or flocks in evidence, such as Slade had passed on his way from the west. There were more big spreads to the east and north, he knew.

With the sun almost to the horizon, they aproached a tight little adobe. There was a small but well-built barn and other outbuildings. The fields surrounding it were in an excellent state of cultivation, the growing crops the best Slade had as yet seen. He remarked on the fact to Felipe.

"My neighbors plant the same thing for too long." Cardena replied. "They wear out the land. Each year I change my planting."

"Crop rotation," Slade nodded. "You have vision, Felipe."

"Were there more rain I would get really good results," the old man said. "Water is the problem here."

"Yes, water," Slade repeated thoughtfully.

"Capitan, if you will enter the house and blow up the fire, which should still be smoldering, I will care for the caballo and the mulo," Felipe suggested.

"That'll be fine," Slade agreed. "Go along with him, Shadow, he's okay."

"I'm sure he understood what you said," chuckled Cardena.

"He did," Slade said. "Otherwise he'd have taken your arm off when you reached for the bridle."

Old Felipe chuckled again and led the horse and the

mule to the barn. Slade opened the cabin door and stepped through it, and looked into the muzzle of a gun not three feet from his face. Behind the gun was the triumphantly grinning face of Cale Brandon.

2

"ELEVATE!" BRANDON SNAPPED. "Get 'em up—slow. Figured you'd be coming here. Up!"

Slade raised his hands, slowly, palms outward, the index fingers pointing to the front.

Brandon's eyes instinctively followed those pointing fingers for an instant; and in that instant Slade's foot moved in a vicious upward kick. The toe of his boot caught Brandon's wrist and slammed his hand upward. The gun exploded before it dropped from Brandon's numbed fingers. The bullet whistled over Slade's head.

Slade hit him, his fist crashing against Brandon's jaw like the smack of a butcher's cleaver on a side of beef. Brandon fell, half stunned by the force of the blow.

"Felipe," Slade called, without turning his head, "fetch that quirt from my saddle pouch; I told you it might come in handy."

"Si, Capitan," replied Cardena, who was running to the cabin, shouting his alarm. A moment later he returned with the whip.

Brandon had gotten his addled senses together and was glaring up at Slade in baffled fury.

"Okay, Felipe, lay on," Slade directed, gesturing to the prostrate man.

Grinning, Felipe brought the leash whistling through the air. Brandon yelled as it curled around his ribs. He yelled again as a second blow ripped the thin fabric of his shirt.

"I'll kill you!" he bawled. "I'll kill you!"

"Lay on, Felipe," Slade said.

His grin widening, Felipe obeyed. Brandon howled. He howled louder as Felipe really got his arm in and the fourth blow spurted blood.

"That'll do," Slade said. "I just wanted him to get a taste of how it feels to be whipped. All right, Brandon, fork your bronk and get going, and be thankful you're still alive. If you pull a gun on me again, I'll kill you. Get going!"

15

He watched Brandon retrieve his horse from where he had hidden it back of the barn and ride off, mingling groans and curses.

"Guess that'll hold him for a while," he told Felipe. He picked up Brandon's fallen gun and handed it to the old man.

"A good iron," he commented. "Keep it for a souvenir, and if those hellions come fooling around again, use it."

"*Capitan*, how did you disarm him?" Felipe asked wonderingly.

"He stood too close when he had the drop on me," Slade explained. "I distracted his attention for a moment and he got a kick on the wrist and a punch on the jaw. Poisonous and snake-blooded, but rather stupid. Incidentally, I was about as stupid. I should have known the hellion might try to pull something. I should have been on my guard. Instead, I walked into the trap like a dumb yearling. Shrewd, in his way, too. Sent the others on to town, figuring that four horses, to say nothing of a wounded man, might kick up a racket and give the thing away. Yes, shrewd, but a mite slow with the think tank."

"But he and those with him are dangerous," Felipe said in worried tones. "You must have a care, *Capitan*."

"I will," Slade promised cheerfully. "Now I'll get the fire going while you finish with the horses."

Felipe proved to be an excellent cook and soon they sat down to an appetizing meal. Slade made a splendid dinner and then, fully fed and content, he rolled a cigarette and smoked it slowly with his last cup of coffee.

"You will spend the night, *Capitan?*" Felipe asked. Slade shook his head.

"*Gracias*," he declined the invitation, "but I'd like to make it to Laredo tonight. There's a moon and it will be pleasant riding. And now I want you to spread the word to your neighbors to hang on to their land. Don't move away, don't sell. There's something queer going on in this section. I don't know what it is, but I aim to find out. Tell them to stick together and fight; they'll have backing they don't expect."

"I will do so," Felipe promised, "And with *El Halcon* here, they will do as he says.

"But do not think too lightly of Brandon and those

with him," he added. "They are *muy malo* men and will be out to even the score."

Slade was willing to agree that Cale Brandon and his associates were indeed "very bad men," but he was not particularly perturbed; he'd outfaced bad men before.

After helping clean up the kitchen, Slade got the rig on Shadow and rode from the cabin, promising Felipe to visit him soon. He rode south by slightly east at a good pace, rejoicing in the beauty of the night.

It was a beautiful night. The glimmering trail below, the luminous heaven above, a glorious canopy from whence shone a myriad stars filling the still dark with their soft, mysterious glow. A warm, autumn night full of a great hush, a stillness wherein no wind stirred and upon whose deep silence distant sounds such as the lonely, hauntingly beautiful plaint of a hunting wolf seemed magnified and rose, clear and plain, above the rhythmic drumming of Shadow's hoofs.

Gradually another cluster of stars came into view, low-lying stars on a level with his vision. Stars that were more golden than the scintillating sparks in the vast vault of the heavens. Stars that steadily grew in size and brightness, the lights of Laredo on the Rio Grande.

Slade knew that Laredo was one of the first settlements in Texas not established as a presidio or a mission. It was the sixth to be founded along the lower Rio Grande, and the second community on the north bank of the river. More than two centuries before, Don Jose de Escandon, Count of Sierra Gorda, colonizer of the region for the King of Spain, and Tomas Sanchez, Spanish nobleman and soldier of fortune, stood on the south bank of the river and gazed north.

"Here," said Don Jose, "is a site suitable for a settlement."

"Your Excellency is right," replied Sanchez. "Here will be a means of communication between New Spain (Mexico) and the outer provinces (Texas). From here roads will run from Monclova, Dolores, La Bahia, San Antonio de Bexar and Revilla. The town will be important, and it will grow. And we will name it Laredo, in honor of the town where Your Excellency was born."

"And the river?" said Don Jose. "Truly it is a great river. What shall we name that?"

Sanchez chuckled. "You have already named it, Your Excellency. It is the Rio Grande."

"And I will appoint you captain of the settlement," said Don Jose.

"I will build a settlement, and maintain a ferry for the convenience of traffic and the royal service," said Sanchez.

"Agreed," answered Don Jose. "And I will grant you fifteen *sitios de ganado mayor* (fifteen square leagues of ranchland) as your reward."

Sanchez, who in Spain had been a rancher in a small way, smiled happily. Already he envisioned the grasslands to the north and east dotted with fat cattle.

"Agreed," he said.

"Come, let us go," chuckled Don Jose. "Today we have named a river and a town. It is enough."

In May, 1755, with three or four families, Tomas Sanchez formally founded Villa de Laredo. The settlement prospered, and two years later, included eleven families numbering eighty-five persons.

The settlement grew steadily in population and importance and at the turn of the eighteenth century the residents numbered more than a thousand.

Laredo's history was one of turbulence. Armies marched and counter-marched through its streets. Laredo watched thousands of gold-hungry immigrants pass along the Rio Grande route to the California gold fields. They stopped at Laredo to rest and replenish their supplies, and Laredo boomed. Some decided there was greater opportunity in the Rio Grande town than they might find in California and settled there.

The expected advent of two railroads, one from Corpus Christi, the other from Mexico, would put an end to Laredo's isolation and open a large part of the Mexican markets to Texas. When Walt Slade rode in that autumn night, Laredo was an optimistic community and plenty woolly.

Slade had visited Laredo before and was familiar with the town's layout. There was a small hotel on Montezuma Street that was favored by cattlemen, where he would attract no attention. Nearby was a reliable stable which would accommodate Shadow. He headed for the stable first and made sure that all the big black's wants were provided for. Then he registered for a room at the hotel.

It was late, but the denizens of Laredo, a large portion of them, at least, apparently paid scant attention to the hands of the clock. They were out in force, on the streets, in the various places of entertainment.

Outside the hotel, Slade hesitated over deciding which way to go. Oh, well, the best place to obtain information was a saloon. Right across the street was one that apparently had been named for the street, or vice-versa. Anyhow, "The Montezuma" was lettered across its plate glass window. And the racket coming over the swinging doors hinted that perhaps the ancient Aztec emperor had come back to life and was throwing a shindig to celebrate his reincarnation. Slade decided to give The Montezuma a whirl. Pushing back the doors, he entered.

The Montezuma was decidedly more ornate than the average cattle-country saloon. The mirror-blazing back bar was pyramided with bottles of every shape and color. The short-skirted, low-cut dresses of the dance floor girls were of excellent material. The long bar was a good imitation of mahogany and highly polished. The stacked dishes on the lunch counter were spotless and shining. The roulette wheels were decorated and bright. The Mexican orchestra was in costume. And the bartenders actually wore coats.

The patrons, however, were more typical of a town that was primarily rangeland but with other and diversified interests. There were plenty of cowhands in the garb of their calling, and Mexicans in black velvet ornamented with much silver. Townspeople were well and conservatively dressed. Altogether, The Montezuma had a prosperous look and appeared to be orderly. However, Slade shrewdly suspected that it could be plenty salty at times; most Border-country saloons were.

Slade's entrance aroused no coment, although he noted that several heads turned in a swift, appraising glance. Quite likely there were gentlemen present who took cognizance of any stranger.

Sipping the drink served him by a pleasantly smiling bartender, Slade studied the gathering and arrived at two conclusions. First, that The Montezuma's clientele was distinctly cosmopolitan. Second, that it was patronized by the more affluent citizens of the town and the surrounding section. At the gaming tables were a number of men who were undoubtedly prosperous ranchowners. And individuals in "store clothes" who were very probably merchants or tradesmen.

Suddenly Slade's eyes narrowed. Sitting at a table near a window, playing poker, was Cale Brandon. He sat bolt upright in his chair, rather stiffly, and Slade noted with a grin that when he leaned back he straightened again, abruptly, and winced. Evidently the whip wielded by the hand of Felipe Cardena had left a mite of soreness.

Five men and Brandon made up the game. Two, Slade concluded, were ranchers; two more, no doubt, local shopkeepers.

The fifth who sat with his back to the window was outstanding. He was tall and broad-shouldered. His hair was tawny and inclined to curl, his features large and regular. At that distance Slade could not determine the color of his eyes. His hands were slender, with long, prehensile fingers. He wore a long black coat that was a perfect fit, a black string tie and a ruffled shirt, immaculately white. His garb, indeed, was somewhat akin to that favored by the gambling fraternity, but Slade quickly decided that he was something more than a card sharp; there was a dignity to him and a distinguished air alien to the wooden-faced followers of the fickle goddess of chance.

The bartender, a congenial soul, noted the direction of Slade's glance.

"Quite a game over there tonight," he observed. "Some up-and-comin' fellers in it. Those two cowmen own big spreads over to the east and north. The two short fellers are partners of Thompson's General Store. The big, tall, good looking gent is Lawyer Danver Wilton Danver. Come over from New Orleans last year and started practicin' here. He's smart and has won some tough cases. Wouldn't be surprised if he gets to be a judge; folks like him. A real gent. The other feller is Cale Brandon. Runs a real estate office. He's sort of top man of the Land Committee. Plenty salty, I've a notion."

"The Land Committee?" Slade said. "What's that?"

"It's made up of fellers who say all the valley land hereabouts had oughta be state land and put up for sale. They been buyin' some the last few months."

The bartender glanced around and lowered his voice.

"That is, if you can say scarin' fellers away or *persuadin'* 'em to sell mighty cheap is buyin'. And sometimes they've got the courts to rule that those old Spanish grants ain't what they should be and that the fellers who hold 'em ain't no better than nesters.

"Not that I'm sayin' what's the right or wrong of it," he added hastily, glancing around again. "Sometimes I figure I talk too darn much."

Slade turned and let the full force of his steady eyes rest on the barkeep's face.

"I don't think a square man has to worry about anything he has to say," he observed quietly.

The bartender looked grateful. "Guess you're right," he agreed, "but sometimes even a square jigger can get into trouble for not tightening the latigo on his jaw."

"Depends on whom he's talking to," Slade said.

"Guess that's right, too," nodded the other. Suddenly his teeth flashed in a grin. "And I ain't worryin' a darn bit about what I've been saying just now."

"Thank you," Slade replied. "And you don't need to worry. But I'll agree with you that talking too much when the wrong pair of ears happens to be listening, isn't always good. Don't forget that."

"I won't," the drink juggler promised as he moved away to wait on a customer.

A moment later, the barkeep remarked to the owner, John Gorty, "That big feller up toward the end of the bar 'pears to be a right hombre, but he's a puzzler. He just asks a question that don't seem to mean much and looks at you, and 'fore you know it you're spillin' your guts. I was sorta curious about him, like I am with all new folks who come in, 'specially folks as outstandin' lookin' as he is, and figured to draw him out a bit. All of a sudden it came to me that I'd been talkin' a bluestreak and he hadn't said nothin'. Didn't say anything at all 'cept a few words, but what he did say I won't forget. Yep, he's a puzzler."

A conclusion that wiser people than the head bartender of The Montezuma had drawn about Walt Slade.

Meanwhile, Slade kept studying the men at the poker table. Cale Brandon frowned at his cards, growled when he lost, grinned when he won. Slade had a notion he would be a bad loser if the luck really ran against him. Which was something he put in the back of his mind for future reference. He had learned from experience that when a man gambled, his true nature would come to the fore, and that a bad loser often lacked judgment when events weren't shaping up to his liking.

He wondered if the other players were regular associates of Brandon's. Perhaps so, but not necessarily. A gaming table brings together men who often have very little else in common. Brandon looked to be, or to have been, a cowman. The two ranchers might have been old acquaintances before he quit following a cow's tail and got into the real estate business.

The lawyer, Wilton Danver, intrigued him. Danver had the look of an able and an adroit man and very likely was. Also a man who would fit into any gathering and be at home anywhere. Danver would probably argue a case in court with the same quiet dignity and reserve with which he played his cards, taking whatever fate had to offer with nonchalance and self-control.

Desiring to get a little closer look at the game and the players, Slade spotted a vacant table nearby. He finished his drink and sauntered toward it. He had nearly reached it when in the darkness outside the open window he saw a shadow of movement. A hand holding a gun was thrust through the window, and the gun was pointed squarely at Wilton Danver's back.

3

SLADE DREW and shot. The gun clattered on the floor. The hand jerked back out of sight. A yelp of pain sounded from the darkness. Slade fired again and bounded forward. When he reached the window he heard fast steps dimming away in the darkness.

The saloon was in an uproar. Men were cursing, shouting questions. The dance floor girls were shrieking. Somebody had fallen through the bass drum and the drummer was screeching outraged Spanish.

"I saw it all!" the bartender yelled above the din. "The hellion aimed to kill Mr. Danver. He'd have drilled him dead center if it hadn't been for that big feller. And was that shootin'! Never seen anything like it!"

The poker players were on their feet. Wilton Danver had whirled around, the fingers of his left hand gripping the left lapel of his long coat. His eyes, which Slade now saw were so deeply blue as to seem black, evidently took in the situation at a glance. His hand dropped to his side, his gaze rested on Slade's face.

"Thank you," he said simply. Slade nodded.

Cale Brandon, his face flushed, was hammering the table. "One of those blasted saddle-colored nesters!" he stormed.

Danver spoke again, addressing Slade. "You saw him, sir? Was he a Mexican?"

"Well, if he was, he'd recently painted his hand white," Slade drawled his reply. This time it was Danver who nodded. Cale Brandon started to bawl something else when he apparently really saw Slade for the first time. His mouth dropped open and he stared. Slade's lips quirked in a grin.

"Looks like I made a mite of a mistake, Brandon, when I said the next time I shot at a hand I'd miss," he remarked in pleasantly conversational tones.

Brandon glared, but did not answer. Wilton Danver glanced curiously from one to the other.

"You know Mr. Brandon?" he asked Slade.

23

"We have—met," *El Halcon* replied.

A little pucker apeared between Danver's brows, but he did not pursue the conversation further.

"Well, boys,' he said, "guess we might as well get back to our game. And thank you again, sir," he said to Slade. "I'll not forget it." With a smile and a nod he sat down and drew his chair up to the table. The others followed suit, but Slade could see that the ranchers and the shop-keepers were a bit shaken by what had happened. Cale Brandon loked somewhat like a fish that had just been jerked out of the water.

Changing his mind about sitting at the table, Slade turned and strolled back to the bar. The place was quiet-ing down. Admiring glances were cast in Slade's direction and heads drew together. The bartender, with a hand that shook a trifle, placed a filled glass before him.

"On the house," he announced. "Mr. Gorty, the boss, said for you to polish off the whole bottle if you're of a mind to, with another one coming up when this one is empty."

"I've a notion this one will be ample," Slade smiled reply. The barkeep nodded.

"Gorty would have felt mighty bad if something had happened to Mr. Danver," he said. "He's one of our best customers, and okay. Gorty's coming over to thank you for what you did. Here he comes now."

John Gorty was a big man with flesh on him. He was past middle age and had a pleasant smile.

"Would like to shake hands, feller," he announced. "That was quick thinking on your part as well as quick shooting. Lots of jiggers with fast gunhands, but they've usually got slow brains. Know just what to do when they're personally involved, but otherwise the wheels turn over just a mite slow. That's been my experience and I've known quite a few. Fill 'em up, Tim, we'll have this one together, all three of us."

"I feel the need of one," said Tim as he replenished Slade's partly emptied glass and filled two more to the brim. "Still got the shakes. Did you send for the sheriff, John?"

"That's right," nodded Gorty. "He should be here any minute. Figured he oughta know about it," he explained to Slade. "Maybe he can run down the sidewinder. Imagine he's got a busted-up hand and may go looking for a doctor."

"Possibly," Slade conceded, although he personally did not think so.

"My name's Gorty, as I reckon Tim told you," the saloonkeeper said. "I don't believe I caught your handle."

Slade supplied it and they shook hands again; he concluded that he liked John Gorty.

"Here comes Sheriff Medford, now," Gorty exclaimed, gesturing to a lean old frontiersman with a lined face and faded but alert blue eyes who had just entered.

Slade knew Sheriff Tobe Medford very well, but his countenance remained impassive as Gorty introduced them, and the sheriff was also poker-faced as they shook hands.

"Figure you did the hellion much damage?" he asked of Slade, after listening to a vivid recital by Gorty, ably seconded by the bartender. Slade shook his head.

"He hightailed down the alley too fast to have been much hurt," he replied. "Maybe skinned his hand a bit, judging from the way he yelped."

"And you didn't get a look at him?"

"All I saw clearly was his hand," Slade replied. "The rest was just a vague shadow of movement that attracted my attention before he stuck the gun in the window."

"Well, you did a mighty good chore, as—as might be expected of—a feller like you," declared Medford. "Everybody would have felt bad if something had happened to Wilton Danver. Guess I'll amble out and scout around a bit, might learn something. Yes, I will have a drink before I go, John."

"Here's the gun Mr. Slade shot out of the sidewinder's hand, one of the boys picked it up and gave it to me," said Gorty.

Medford took it, gave it a glance and passed it to Slade, with an inquiring glance. The ranger examined it carefully.

"Regulation Colt forty-five, but with the sight filed down," he commented. "Looks like I got the hellion across the top of his hand; no bullet mark on the gun." He passed the weapon back to Gorty.

"Hope you took the whole back off," grunted the sheriff. "Keep it for a souvenir, John. Uh-huh, a 'for hire' gun. But why the devil did he try to shoot Danver, and in the back?"

Slade shrugged. "That's your question," he countered, "and you know the section and conditions here better than I do."

"Well, I can't answer it," growled Medford. "Wouldn't have figured Danver to have an enemy; everybody likes him. But I reckon you never know what enemies a feller may have made. He's a lawyer, and I gather he was an assistant prosecutor for a while over in Louisiana; could have been some hellion he got sent up for a stretch, who held a grudge and figured to even up the score."

"Could be," Slade conceded.

"I'll go over and talk to him a minute," Medford said, adding, "Now if it had been Cale Brandon I could understand it better. Brandon is always stepping on somebody's toes. Oh, he's all right, but he's sure got a knack for settin' folks by the ears. Been that way ever since he set up in business here."

"Brandon isn't from this section?" Slade asked.

"Came from up in the Panhandle, I understand," Medford replied. "Heard he owned a little spread up around Amarillo, sold it at a profit and bought another one and sold it. That got him interested in the real estate business, he said, and he decided to branch out a bit. Finally ended up here and has been buying up land. Owns quite a block in the valley now. Smart enough, all right, but all out for himself. Square enough in his dealings, from all I've heard, but don't let any grass grow under his feet. Reckon you've met the sort."

"Yes," Slade admitted dryly. "Quite a few of them."

Sheriff Medford shot him a quick glance, but asked no questions.

"Drop in and see me when you have time, if you aim to coil your twine here for a spell," he said. "Well, I'll have a word with Danver before I leave."

As the sheriff walked away, Gorty studied the poker game. "I wonder," he remarked thoughtfully, "I wonder if the hellion could have been after Brandon instead of Danver? They're about the same size. Danver is a mite taller, but one's as broad as the other and Danver was settin' with his back sort of slantwise to the window and his face in the shadow. Jigger could have easily mistaken

one for t'other. I've a notion quite a few folks would sort
of like to take a shot at Brandon. I wonder, now."

"Not impossible," Slade conceded. He had himself been
entertaining something of the same notion, for he could
well believe that there were people who would take pleasure in killing Cale Brandon. Although, he felt that who-
ever attempted the deed would have spotted his victim
carefully and marked just where he was sitting. Not
necessarily so, however. And there was also a chance that
the two men might have changed chairs earlier in the
evening. Brandon looked to be the sort who would put
credence in the gambler's superstition that changing
chairs in a game will change one's luck. And Danver
would have no doubt humored him if he requested a
change of seats.

All conjecture, pro and con, but in the circumstances,
all angles should be explored. No matter who was the intended victim, a premeditated, snake-blooded killing had
narrowly been averted. And as a law enforcement officer,
Slade was interested in dropping a loop on the offender
no matter whom he had in mind when he lined sights
with Wilton Danver's back.

"Wonder why the sidewinder didn't stand back in the
dark and shoot instead of risking shoving his hand through
the window?" Gorty questioned.

"As you said yourself, Danver was sitting with his back
slantwise to the window, and with his face and his body,
too, in the shadow," Slade pointed out. "Guess he figured
he wouldn't be taking much of a chance of being de-
tected. If I hadn't been looking straight at the window at
just that moment, I would have very likely not noticed
what was going on in time to prevent it."

"And I've a darn good notion most anybody else
wouldn't have noticed in time if he'd been looking right
straight at where the hand came in," Gorty observed
dryly. Slade smiled and did not comment.

Sheriff Medford finished his conversation with Danver
and turned away. Cale Brandon pushed back his chair,
rose to his feet and overtook the sheriff, touching him on
the shoulder; Medford turned to face him. Slade could
see Brandon's lips moving but could not hear what was
said. He did see the sheriff slant a glance in his direction
and nod his head. Brandon appeared to be urging some

course of action; there was tentative agreement in the sheriff's nod. However, whatever it was, he did not at once put in effect, but with a deprecating wave of his hand left the saloon, shooting Slade one swift and significant glance. Brandon went back to his game and Slade thought his face wore a smug expression.

Slade had a very good notion as to what Brandon told the sheriff and his lips quirked in a smile of amusement. At an opportune time the sheriff would probably denounce El Halcon and issue a stern warning that he be on his good behaviour while sojourning in the sheriff's bailiwick. Trust Tobe Medford to put it across.

"Tobe's all right," remarked Gorty. "Yep, he's okay, and a square man. I know he ain't been overly pleased about some of the things that have been happening hereabouts of late, but the politicians have an in with the courts and over to the capital and Tobe's been sort of hamstrung in trying to straighten things out. Cale Brandon and his bunch sort of have an in with the politicians and are able to get by with plenty."

"Wonder what Brandon and his bunch have in mind?" Slade asked casually. Gorty shook his head.

"Hard to figure," he replied. "The land they've been buying up sure ain't very valuable. Of course, when the railroad comes through from Corpus Christi the land along the right-of-way will be worth more than it is now, but I can't see the valley land going up to amount to anything. It'll be just the same—arid cattle land and not especially good, for even cows. You have to amble east a ways before you hit good grazing ground. They've got something in mind, all right, but darned if I know what. Maybe just pure cussedness and not liking Mexicans and nesters, as they call the little farmers who try to grow something on a patch. As to that, I can't say."

"Doesn't seem likely that they'd go in for such an elaborate project just for spite," Slade commented.

"Doesn't look that way," Gorty agreed. "Well, I've got some chores to do. Have another drink?"

"Thanks, but if you don't mind I think I'll sit down at that vacant table over there and have some coffee and a sandwich," Slade replied.

"Sure," said Gorty. "I'll have 'em sent over." With a smile and a nod he hurried off. Slade sauntered to the table and sat down where he had a view of the poker game. Wilton Danver was almost facing him, and he had a good profile view of Cale Brandon.

Danver was certainly a fine looking man, poised, dignified. His mouth was tight but shapely, his thin lips barely moving when he spoke, his blue eyes very keen, very clear, and very masterful. Cool as a dead snake, too; the near-successful attempt on his life didn't cause him to turn a hair. A quiet, self-possessed and dangerous man. Slade didn't miss the thumb and fingers gripping the left lapel of his coat when he turned from the table—the unmistakeable gesture of the shoulder-holster pull; there was a gun under that long black coat. Nothing unusual about that, however; nearly everybody in this section packed a gun, even folks who didn't know how to use one. Which latter category, Slade was pretty well convinced, did not include Wilton Danver. He dismissed the lawyer who, while interesting as a character study, was divorced from the problem at hand, and turned his attention to Cale Brandon.

Another dangerous man—dangerous in the fashion of the sidewinder, the pygmy rattlesnake of the desert that strikes from cover without warning. Cale Brandon was not the sort it was wise to turn one's back to.

He wondered just what was the scheme apparently maturing in Brandon's sneaky mind. Brandon didn't look to have the intelligence to maneuver anything really intricate and important, but outward appearances could be deceptive. His stratagem of holing up in Felipe Cardena's cabin denoted imagination, cunning and initiatve. Brandon could well be a lot smarter than he looked to be. Well, he'd find out about that, sooner or later.

Slade finshed his coffee and sandwich, lighted a cigarette and smoked in leisurely comfort. Pinching out the butt, he rose to his feet. Tobe Medford's parting glance had hinted at a hankering for a gabfest and he determined to drop in at his office before going to bed. Waving to Gorty, he left the saloon.

4

THE SHADE WAS drawn when Slade reached the sheriff's office, but light seeped through the cracks. He mounted the steps and knocked on the door. Medford's gruff voice bade him enter.

"Lock the door," the sheriff directed, gesturing to a chair. "Well, Walt, what the devil brings you here?"

"Guess you know," Slade replied, sitting down and beginning the manufacture of another cigarette.

"Yes, I guess I do," Medford grunted. "And I'm darn glad you're here," he added. "Things are getting out of control."

"So I gather," Slade conceded. "Just what's the answer?"

"I wish I knew," growled the sheriff. "The whole blasted business don't seem to make sense, but there's enough of some sort of a reason back of it to cause a lot of wire-pulling all the way from here to the capital. Local politicians appear to be answering to hints from Austin and lining up behind the blasted Land Committee in their efforts to get control of the valley. I've tried to get to the bottom of the business but all I get is evasive answers and reminders that the coming of the railroad from Corpus Christi will make the valley land valuable, which it won't, in my opinion."

"Your opinion is correct," Slade said. "The railroad is coming, all right, and there's another building up from Mexico which should reach here a year or so later than the Corpus Christi line. They'll put an end to Laredo's isolation and open up the Mexican markets to Texas. As a result, the town will boom, but the valley lands will not be affected. No, it isn't the coming of the railroads they have in mind; it's something else. What it is, I must find out."

"If the hellions were acquiring land by legitimate means it would be okay," said the sheriff, "but they're not. They're using intimidation, legal skullduggery, and even force. The Texas-Mexicans are scared to talk, knowing

30

that if they do they'll just make more trouble for themselves. Meanwhile the real Mexicans in Nuevo Laredo across the river are getting sore as blazes over what's being done to their blood kin. Until this thing started there was the friendliest relations between the two towns, but now that's a thing of the past."

"In that is the making of real trouble," Slade replied gravely. "Liable to end up paralleling what happened in Brownsville back in the 'Fifties. The same sort of practices were put in effect there by unscrupulous politicians. It gave the bandit leader Juan Nepomucebo Cartinas—Cheno Cartinas he was called—opportunity to stage raids across the river, presumably espousing the cause of his oppressed 'countrymen.' He actually captured Brownsville in a surprise raid and held the city captive for forty-eight hours, incidentally killing quite a few people. Only with the help of Mexican regulars from Matamoros across the Rio Grande, in much the same position to Brownsville as Nuevo Laredo is to Laredo, was something like order restored. But by his act, Cartinas had recruited many followers on both sides of the river and continued his raiding and cattle stealing until the rangers finally drove him back to Mexico and kept him there. We don't want something similar to happen here."

"We sure don't," agreed Medford.

"And now," Slade said, "I've got something to tell you."

In detail, he related his experience with Cale Brandon. The sheriff swore pungently.

"That ornery, snake-blooded blankety-blank!" he concluded. "Is Cardena going to put a charge against the so-and-so?"

Slade shook his head. "Wouldn't do any good, in the circumstances," he replied. "I wouldn't be an effective witness without revealing my ranger connections, which I don't want to do at present."

"Going to remain El Halcon for a while, eh?"

"That's right," Slade answered. "By the way, I suppose Brandon slipped you the word that I'm El Halcon?"

"Uh-huh," nodded Medford. "Told me I'd oughta run you out of the section. I said I would if you gave me reason to do so, but that so far as I knew, nobody could ever find a reason for asking you to move on. Incidentally, you made a powerful friend when you kept Wilton Danver from getting his comeuppance. Danver hasn't been here very long, but already he packs influence and is tieing onto more all the time. He might come in handy."

"I've thought of that," Slade agreed. "Will keep it in mind. He appears to know Brandon."

"Most everybody knows Brandon," Medford grunted. "Especially anyone who likes to play poker. He's a steady gambler. So is Danver, for that matter, only Danver just plays for reaxation whlile Brandon plays for keeps; he's really got the gambling fever."

"So I gathered," Slade observed thoughtfully. "And he may be gambling for mighty big stakes."

"Meaning?"

"Meaning," Slade explained, "that whatever is in the making hereabouts is likely to be big. I've a feeling it is. And so far as we know, Brandon appears to be the big he-wolf of the pack."

"Yeah, I guess he's that, all right," Medford conceded. "I sure wish I'd seen old Felipe quirting him; bet he bellered like blazes."

"He did," Slade smiled, "louder than Felipe did when he was being whipped."

Medford chuckled, but was immediately grave again. "The hellion is liable to take it out on Felipe, though," he said.

"I've thought of that, and I figure to take precautions," Slade replied, "I think I'll take a little ride through the valley tomorrow."

"And maybe you can learn something," suggested the sheriff. "Somehow I feel the darn railroads have something to do with it. Indirectly, of course."

"Not impossible, although for the life of me, I can't figure what," Slade said. "I may take a ride to the railroad shortly, it's not so very far off, now. Have a little talk with the engineers who are running the line; they might know something."

"A good idea," the sheriff nodded. "You can talk their language."

Which was true. Shortly before the death of his father, following financial reverses that cost the elder Slade his ranch, Walt Slade had graduated from a famous school of engineering. He had intended to take a postgraduate course to round out his education and better fit him for the profession he had determined to make his life work. That, for the time, became impossible, and when Captain Jim McNelty, the famous commander of the Border Battalion, suggested that he come into the rangers for a while and study in spare time, Slade, who had worked some with Captain Jim during summer vacations, thought the notion a good one. Long since, he had gotten more from private study than he could have hoped for from the postgrad; but ranger work had gotten a strong hold on him and he was loath to sever connections, just yet, with the illustrious body of law enforcement officers. He was young and there was plenty of time to be an engineer. He would stick with the rangers for a while.

His knowledge of engineering had often come in handy in the course of his ranger activities and had helped him solve some unusual mysteries.

Due to his habit of working undercover as much as possible, he had built up a dual reputation. Those who knew the truth declared him the ablest and most fearless of the rangers. Others, including some puzzled sheriffs and marshals, who knew him only as El Halcon, were wont to insist that he was just a blasted owlhoot too smart to get caught but who would get his comeuppance sooner or later. Which last worried Captain McNelty, who more than once protested the peril involved in allowing this misconception to persist.

"Some trigger-happy sheriff or deputy will feed you a dose of lead poisoning, thinking he's doing the right thing," said Captain Jim. "Or some darned outlaw out to get a reputation as a fast gunhand may take a chance on shooting you in the back to help him get it."

"Could be," Slade agreed cheerfully, "but as El Halcon there are avenues of information open to me that would be closed to a known peace officer. Also, outlaws who figure me to just be one of their kind horning in on their preserves sometimes get careless and tip their hand. You know it's been done. Of course, sir, if you insist—"

"Oh, go ahead and commit suicide if you've got a

hankering to," Captain Jim would growl. "Far be it from
me to stop you if that's the way you feel about it, but,
blankety-blank it—be careful!"

Slade wasn't particularly careful and went his carefree
way, confident that right would prevail, which so far it
had, to the discomfiture of a number of gentlemen of
easy conscience who thought they could make crime pay.

Sheriff Medford glanced at his watch. "Getting pretty
late, but I feel like a nightcap before going to bed," he
announced. "What say we drop over to The Montezuma?"

"I can stand another cup of coffee," Slade agreed.
"Let's go."

"May be a good notion for us to go in together this
way," Medford chuckled. "Will give folks the idea that
I'm sort of keeping tabs on you and maybe putting a
bug in your ears as to how you behave yourself. I'll try
to look salty."

"You won't have to try very hard," Slade smiled.

There was a decided turning of heads when they entered The Montezuma together. Slade considered it quite
probable that the word that El Halcon was in town had
been pretty well spread around. Medford suppressed a
grin.

"The gabbers are hard at it," he said as they sat down
and gave their order. "They're putting two and two
together and making eight or nine. Looks like the poker
game busted up. Don't see Brandon anywhere. Usually
find him at the bar after the play is over. Maybe his back
don't feel too good. Or his wrist, either. Imagine that's
a mite sore, too. You took one heck of a chance, kicking
the gun out of his hand that way."

"I played football in college," Slade replied, with a
smile.

"Uh-huh, but a pigskin and a hunk of lead are two
different things," grunted the sheriff. "Watch out for
him, Walt, he's bad. And I've got a notion he don't
lack for brains. Figuring up a scheme like what it looks
as if he's working on, whatever the devil it is, means
something in the think tank."

"Yes, if the scheme, whatever it is, is wholly his,"
Slade remarked thoughtfully. "He may have help from
some source we don't know about."

"That's true," the sheriff conceded, "but he sure don't

hang out with anybody, so far as I know, that would fit into the picture. The rest of the Land Committee are a pretty grubby lot. He may have connections, though, over at the capital."

"He has connections with a different element, too," Slade said. "I feel pretty sure those three hellions with him at the whipping aren't members of the committee, at least so far as public consumption goes. They are hired guns or I miss my guess. Typical Border scum that would do for their own mothers if the price was right. The one I shot in the hand was the sort that evolved from the snake instead of the monkey, putting an erroneous interpretation on the Darwinian theory of evolution."

"You talk like a blasted dictionary," grumbled the sheriff, "but I guess I gather what you mean—he's got his share of sidewinder blood."

"Something like that," Slade agreed. "Anyhow, he was an unsavory character."

"You don't figure it could have been him who tried to shoot Danver through the window?"

Slade shook his head. "No, for he would have had to use his left hand, and the angle at which the gun came through the window rejects that possibility."

"You don't miss much, do you?" said the sheriff.

"It is a primary precept of the rangers not to overlook any detail, no matter how apparently insignificant," Slade replied. "That's one of the fundamental reasons why the rangers are the rangers."

"Guess that's so," agreed the sheriff. "Well, I'm heading for bed.'

"So am I," Slade said. They left the saloon together, eyes following them out the door.

In his room, Slade cleaned and oiled his guns before retiring. "Looks like we're in for some interesting experiences," he told the big Colts. "Sure started off with a bang."

He holstered the sixes, placed them ready to hand and in a few minutes was fast asleep.

5

MEANWHILE CALE BRANDON was walking furtively along Zaragoza Street not far from where the bridge to Nuevo Laredo spanned the turbulent waters of the Rio Grande. He slipped into a shadowy hallway, paused and gazed back the way he had come. Satisfied that he was not wearing a tail, he tiptoed a little farther into the hall and tapped on a door.

"Come in," said a voice.

Brandon opened the door and entered a room lighted only by a wan sliver from a streep lamp seeping through closed shutters.

"Lock the door and sit down," said the voice. The speaker was but a formless blur on the far side of a dimly seen table.

Muttering under his breath, Brandon groped his way to the table, located a chair by feel and sat down.

"Dark in here!" he complained.

"And it's going to stay dark," said the voice. "Too many queer things happening hereabouts all of a sudden to take chances on a light. You sure nobody followed you here?"

"I'm sure," Brandon replied. "I stood in the hall and looked back for quite a while. What's on your mind?"

"Plenty," replied the voice. "Looks like you bungled the Cardena business for fair."

Brandon cut loose with a string of profanity. "How the devil was I to know that infernal *El Halcon* would show up like he did?" he demanded. "And Simpson tried to pull on him!"

"Simpson's an idiot," said the voice. "He's lucky to be alive. I'm glad he paid for his idiocy. And then, or so I gathered from Donley, you couldn't be satisfied to let well enough alone but had to make a try at getting the drop on him. Evidently you didn't. Tell me just what happened, and tell it straight."

Brandon told him, truthfully. "I'll kill the hellion," he concluded, with a vicious oath.

"Better leave him alone," the other advised. "You're not smart enough to buck him. Leave that for somebody who's capable. One thing is certain, his presence here means trouble for us. He has a reputation for taking up for Mexicans, among other things."

"You figure he aims to horn in?"

"Why not?" countered the voice. "If he manages to maneuver things to get us where the hair is short, we'll have to pay through the nose. He has a reputation for that sort of thing, too, and has done it before. I don't intend it to happen here. He's got to be done away with."

"I'll do away with him, if I get the chance," Brandon declared venomously.

"More likely he'll do away with you if you get what you think is a chance," the other said. "From what I've heard of him, I'm inclined to think he's the devil himself. As soon as he shows up in a section, things begin to happen, whether he has anything to do with them or not. That attempted killing in The Montezuma still has to be explained."

"I still say that was a blasted nester trying to pay off a grudge," said Brandon.

"That's not an explanation," said the unseen speaker. "The important question is, why? Anything apparently unexplainable that happens hereabouts could well be tied up in some way with the project we have in mind. And don't forget, *El Halcon* is shrewd, mighty shrewd. He's been known to cook up some very cute schemes and make them look authentic."

"What do you mean by that?" Brandon asked in puzzled tones.

The voice became meditative. "Nothing definite, as yet, but I'm beginning to wonder. What *El Halcon* did would be a nice way to get in good with— a lot of people. Yes, I wonder."

"Yes, it could have been a plant," Brandon agreed thoughtfully. "The gun could have just been dropped to the floor, to make the play look good. I got a look at that gun, Gorty showed it to me; there wasn't any bullet mark on it. Uh-huh, I'm beginning to wonder, too. What are we going to do about that blasted Felipe Cardena?"

"We have got to make an example of Cardena," the other declared with decision. "If he is allowed to get away with what he did, others may summon the courage to do something similar. We can't have that. We've got the nesters pretty well scared and we've got to keep them that way. Only this time try not to bungle it."

Brandon snarled like an angry dog. "I won't," he promised. "I owe Cardena plenty, and I always aim to pay my debts."

"If you'd learn to look at things in a detached way instead of hunting for personal vengeance you'd accomplish more," the other said. "Such an attitude clouds one's judgment, that is, if you have any to cloud, which sometimes I doubt. Now don't go flying off the handle and proving what I just said. Learn to control yourself, Brandon."

The deep breath Brandon drew was audible. "All right," he said, "but if you'd gotten a quirt across your back, maybe you wouldn't feel so smug. Anything else? If not, I'm going to bed."

"Nothing, except leave El Halcon to me," said the other.

"All right," Brandon agreed again, rising to his feet, "but I won't feel right so long as he's running around loose."

"He won't be running around loose for long," the other promised grimly.

6

ALTHOUGH IT WAS LATE when he went to bed, Slade was up early in the morning. After enjoying a leisurely breakfast, he got the rig on Shadow and rode north by west across the valley. When he arrived at Felipe Cardena's adobe he found the old fellow pottering about the stable and received a warm welcome.

"Let us eat," said Felipe. "One can always think and talk better on the full stomach. Ha! The *caballo* remembers me. He also must eat."

"And I'm still enough of a cowhand to be ready to eat at any time," Slade said as he dismounted. "Then I'd like for you to take a little ride with me to visit some of your neighbors."

"It will be the pleasure, *Capitan*, and they will be most glad to welcome you," Felipe replied.

When they sat down to an appetizing meal, Felipe asked a question.

"The Senor Brandon, did you see him in town?"

"He was playing poker in The Montezuma," Slade replied. "Acted like his back was sort of sore."

"Quite likely it was," Felipe chuckled. "I am old, but my arm is still strong. But you must have a care, *Capitan*, he will be out to even the score."

"Doubtless," Slade agreed. "And that goes for you, too, Felipe. If he and his bunch allow you to get away with it, their hold on the valley folks will be weakened. Such an outfit rules by instilling fear. Once the fear is gone, they lose power. So I consider it very likely that they will try to make trouble for you. That's one of the reasons why I want to visit your neighbors. A single stick can be broken easily, but a bundle of them is something else. If the people of the valley can be persuaded to stick together and resist, Brandon and his bunch will find themselves holding the hot end of the branding iron."

"Si," nodded Felipe. "It is true. And now that *El Halcon* is here, the people will grow bold, even those who

39

are not of Mexican blood. They, too, have heard of *El Halcon*, the friend of the lowly."

"I hope you're right," Slade said.

"I am right," Felipe declared. He paused, looking reflective.

"*Capitan*," he said, "there is something you should know. South of the great river there is one who calls himself *El Cascabel*."

"The Rattlesnake," Slade translated. "A name given a great *bandido* of other days."

"*Si*," agreed Felipe, "but that *El Cascabel* was a true man who fought for the people and strove to make an end of tyranny. This *El Cascabel* is different, and he is inciting the people south of the river to violence, calling upon them to aid their blood brothers here to the north."

"And just what is he?" Slade asked.

"He is an outlaw, a bandit leader who seeks only his own advancement, nothing more. The ignorant believe him to be a liberator, but he is not. He is evil and has many evil men at his command. He plans to create turmoil, to burn and loot."

Slade looked grave. "I'd feared something of the sort," he said. "And if the people of the valley join with him and take part in such a scheme, they'll be playing right into Brandon's hands. Now they've got a lot of public opinion on their side, here and in other parts of Texas, but they could quickly change that by allowing themselves to be sucked into such a scheme. Well, that's something else to take care of."

"*El Halcon* will take care of it in quite the proper way," Felipe predicted cheerfully. "Oh, no, *Capitan*, you will not disappoint me and those who trust in you. I have no fear."

"*Gracias, amigo*," Slade replied, his cold eyes abruptly all kindness. "Faith begets faith; we will not fail."

All the long October afternoon Slade and old Felipe rode the valley, pausing at adobes and little farm houses and talking with the inhabitants of the humble dwellings, and when Slade finally headed for Laredo, under the stars, he was highly pleased with the results he had obtained and was confident that Felipe had nothing to fear at the hands of Cale Brandon and his followers.

"We will be prepared and ready," Felipe said. "Aye, we will be ready."

What concerned Slade more was Felipe's account of the bandit leader *El Cascabel* and his activities. The volatile people of Nuevo Laredo and its environs could easily be aroused by such propaganda as he appeared to be spewing forth, and incited to acts of violence. Such things had happened before, and right now was not a good time for them to happen again. Not improbably, such a development might be the torch that would set the whole Border aflame, with rapine and bloodshed the portion on both sides of the river from end to end of Texas. The time was ripe for just such an explosion.

Unfortunate land policies of the government, already being put into effect, promised that millions of Mexicans would lose prescriptive rights to theretofore inalienable communal lands of free villages and would become peons, little better than slaves, on the great *haciendas* which would absorb the erstwhile village lands. And there were rumors that the move on the part of the government had been instigated by powerful influences north of the Rio Grande. Slade believed that under such conditions a great socio-economic upheaval was sooner or later inevitable. Historical developments would prove him right.

The present result of the turmoil in the land of *manana* was that relations between the Border peoples, which had slowly and steadily been becoming more amiable since the close of the Mexican War, were again becoming strained. It wouldn't take much to blow the lid off, and Laredo might well end up being the focus of wrath.

All in all, it looked like he had stumbled onto something that promised to be much more important than anything he had anticipated. What had appeared to be but a commonplace case of nefarious manipulations by crooked promoters could roar into an international conflagration. He was in a somber state of mind when he reached Laredo. Something had to be done to forestall such a calamity, and right now he hadn't the slightest notion as to what that all-important something might be. Feeling the need of a drink and a mite of relaxation, he stabled Shadow and headed for The Montezuma.

Despite the fact that the night was well along, The Montezuma proved to be crowded, and extra noisy. Tim, the head bartender, greeted him effusively and refused to take payment for the drink. "You ain't finished that bottle yet," he reminded. "I got it hid in back. Got to finish that bottle before you can buy a drink. That's Gorty's orders."

"Looks like I'll be drinking free for quite a while," Slade smiled, falling in with the other's humor.

"Uh-huh, you're different from most of these guzzlers," Tim said. "They wouldn't have let go the neck till the darn thing showed white to the bottom. Here's how! One out of my private bottle, too."

They clinked glasses and Tim hurried off to attend to business.

Glancing over the crowd, Slade failed to see Cale Brandon. Neither Sheriff Medford nor Wilton Danver were in evidence. The big poker table next to the window was occupied by a troop of cowhands.

John Gorty came over to pass the time of day. "Glad to see you back," he said. "Hope you'll decide to coil your twine in the section; we can use men like you. Mr. Danver was in for a little while earlier and asked about you. Expressed the hope that you and him would get better acquainted. He's a good man to get in with; up and coming. Nope, I haven't seen Cale Brandon tonight. He's a good one to keep away from, in my opinion, and I've a notion Tobe Medford will agree with me, if you put the question to him. Tobe was here a little while ago. Reckon he's making the rounds of the other places; he usually does on a busy night like this. Be seeing you; got some chores to attend to." He hurried off. Slade sipped his drink and studied the crowd.

Gradually, however, he tired of the unceasing racket, which disturbed his train of thought. He decided to scout around a bit, perhaps run into the sheriff. He said goodnight to Tim and left the saloon.

For some time he sauntered about Laredo's bustling business section, the activity of which seemed never to lessen. He visited quite a few places in quest of the sheriff, and did not find him. Gradually, thinking deeply, he worked his way toward the waterfront section of the town, where it was quietier and not nearly so well-lighted. He knew that near the river, especially on Grant and Zaragoza Streets, were a number of small cantinas patronized largely by Mexicans and cowhands, where he thought he might possibly learn something relative to the activities of the sinister and furtive *El Cascabel*, the bandit leader.

Concentrating on the two-pronged problem which confronted him, he gave less heed to his surroundings than usual and he did not note the stealthy figure that glided along some distance behind him, freezing motionless when he paused, slipping along again when he moved on, always in the shadow, hugging the walls of the buildings.

On Grant Street just west of Bernardo Avenue, Slade paused in front of a dimly-lighted cantina. Over the swinging doors came the sound of soft music and subdued conversation. The sort of place fitted to his mood, he felt. He pushed open the doors and entered. The bar was crowded, chiefly with young Mexicans, and a sprinkling of cowhands. Near the dance floor, Slade spotted a vacant table and sat down. A smiling waiter took his order with a deep bow. Several patrons turned to gaze at him. One or two smiled and bowed. Evidently he was recognized as *El Halcon*.

A moment later, a hulking, beetle-browed individual strolled in, shouldered his way to the bar and bought a drink. Over the rim of his glass he studied the room as reflected in the back bar mirror. His gaze held intently on Slade for an instant. And at the same time the gaze of a slender, very handsome and immaculately dressed young Mexican standing nearby centered on him.

Tossing off his drink, the big man sauntered out. After a moment, the young Mexican also took his departure. Outside the cantina he paused, glancing up and down the street. The big man, walking swiftly, was just turning into Bernardo Avenue. The Mexican followed, almost at a run. Turning the corner, he spotted his quarry walking south toward Zaragoza Street. The Mexican turned the corner into Zaragoza Street close on the heels of the other. There he paused, one dark hand caressing the haft of a heavy throwing knife sheathed at his belt. He saw the man enter a hallway. He crossed the street and strolled carelessly along until he was nearly opposite the hall. In the shadow of an alley mouth, he paused again, and waited.

7

Sipping his drink, Slade gave the cantina a careful once-over. The place was orderly and comparatively quiet. The orchestra's instruments were muted. Two big hanging lamps, one over the dance floor, the other over the bar, shed a soft glow that was restful.

Slade quickly concluded, however, that the place could be explosive. He was familiar with such a gathering—reckless, quick-tempered young vaqueros, many of them from south of the river, and equally reckless cowhands from the spreads to the east, most of them also young. At the moment all was laughter and subdued gaiety, but that could change in the twinkling of an eye.

The dance floor girls were young and pretty. The spangles on their short skirts reflected the light in a kaleidescope of hues as they whirled and pirouetted in the arms of their partners. Not at all bad!

One in particular attracted his attention, a slender, graceful little thing with great sloe eyes. A senorita with no Indian blood. She met his admiring glance and smiled with a flash of little teeth very white against the hibiscus scarlet of her sweetly formed lips. Slade decided that when she was free, a dance with her was in order.

The number ended, her cowhand partner headed for the bar and he was about to approach her when a slender young Mexican entered hurriedly and crossed the room to where she was standing. A low-voiced conversation ensued. Slade was sure he caught a glint of black eyes in his direction. He chuckled. Her amante, no doubt, who perhaps supervised her choice of partners.

The young vaquero said a last word, turned and walked to the bar. He ordered a drink and stood with it untasted in his hand, facing the door. There was a tense alertness in his pose that caused Slade to wonder. He turned as a soft voice sounded at his elbow.

"Capitan," said the little dancer, "you will buy wine?"

"Of course," Slade replied, rising to his feet and pulling out a chair. It was the customary thing to do when a

45

dance floor girl approached. With a bottle of wine she could sit out a number or two.

She accepted the chair, but moved it a little until she was sitting beside him and facing the door.

A waiter brought the wine. The girl raised her glass, smiling gaily, but there was nothing gay in the tones of her voice when she spoke, apparently proposing a toast, as was also customary.

"*Capitan*," she said, "you are in deadly danger. Men come to kill—*El Halcon*. Estaban, who is your friend, just told me."

"Yes?" Slade replied. "He is sure?"

"He is sure," she answered, her eyes never leaving the door.

"How does he know?" Slade asked.

"There was a man who saw you enter. He gazed at you a moment—at your reflection in the back bar—then departed with haste. Estaban knew him to be one who kills for hire. He followed. Now the man has others with him and they come here to slay. At any moment they come."

"Okay," Slade said. "You had better move away."

"I will not," she replied flatly. "Should I flee when danger threatens *El Halcon*, the friend of the lowly?"

Slade shot her a quick smile. "Bueno!" he said. "But be ready to slide to the right and hit the floor when I tell you. Don't forget, now. Otherwise it may be too bad for both of us."

"I won't," she promised. "Look! Estaban signals!"

Slade saw the *vaquero's* hand raise slightly, then drop to the hilt of his big throwing knife. He tensed for instant action.

The swinging doors slammed open. Four men bulged in, fanning out sideways along the wall.

"Move!" Slade snapped. The girl whisked from her chair and hit the floor as she had been told.

Over went the table, Slade behind it. Guns blazed from the doorway. Slugs hammered the thick oak top of the table; one came through, but did no damage. Both of Slade's Colts let go with a rattling crash. A yell echoed the reports. One of the gunmen fell sprawling. A second reeled back against the wall, clutching at his blood-spurting shoulder. A knife buzzed through the air from where the young vaquero stood. Its point thudded into the wall—after passing through the man's throat. Yells outside sounded above the utter pandemonium inside. Three more men rushed in with drawn guns. Things were getting a mite hot.

Too darned hot, Slade thought. He blasted three more shots at the ducking, weaving killers. The muzzles of his Colts tipped up, gushed flame and smoke.

With a clang and jangle of smashed glass and splintered metal, both hanging lamps went out. Darkness swooped down on the wild turmoil like a thrown blanket. Slade rolled to the right and scrambled to his feet.

The little dancer was clutching his arm with both hands. Her voice shrilled above the bedlam of yells, shrieks, booming guns and smashing furniture.

"Follow me! Quick! Quick! Before they cut us off; they're coming this way!"

Apparently, she could see in the dark, for she guided him expertly past smashed chairs and overturned tables, across the dance floor through a door. They crossed a room and another door loomed before them, dimly outlined by street light filtering through a window. The girl grasped the knob.

"It's locked!" she gasped. "I can't open it!"

"Stand aside," Slade told her and hurled his two hundred pounds of muscular weight against the door. It creaked and groaned but stood firm. Once again. A plank splintered. The door sagged from one hinge.

"They're coming!" cried the girl. "I hear them."

Slade hit the door a third time. The second hinge tore free and the door thudded to the ground. They scrambled over it as steps sounded in the room. The girl again led the way, turning to the right .

A gun boomed. The slug came close. Then a scream shivered the night air, rising to a bubbling shriek and chopping off short.

"Estaban always carries two knives," the girl said laconically. "Run!"

"But Estaban—can't leave him," Slade protested, starting to hold back.

"Run!" she repeated. "He follows. Run!"

Slade heard swift, light steps behind them and obeyed orders, chuckling. Despite its deadly seriousness, the whole affair had a humorous side, or so he felt. Then he saved his breath for running, for the little dancer was setting a pace that gave him all he could do to match.

Estaban drew abreast of them; he wasn't even breathing hard.

"Estaban was brought up by the mountain Yaquis, and running is an exercise much practiced by the Yaquis," the girl explained.

"I think you must have been brought up by them, too," Slade panted.

"I'm a dancer," she said, as if no further explanation were necessary.

"At the next alley I turn aside and make the great noise," said Estaban. "Hasten on."

He drew ahead without effort. Slade shook his head and saved his breath. Estaban whipped into a dark opening. As Slade and the girl sped past, a volley of yells and curses in two languages bellowed from the alley, and the banging of a gun.

"That should slow them up, if they really are following," said the girl. "Perhaps they are not, but we can't afford to wait and see. Hasten! I take you where you will be safe."

Slade hadn't the slightest idea where she had in mind, but fervently hoped it wasn't far off; the gruelling pace was beginning to tell a bit. When she turned left into Convent Avenue he began to get a notion. For directly ahead loomed the spidery outlines of the International Bridge.

"Going to cross?" he asked as she slowed her gait a little.

"Yes," she replied. "Over there at the place to which we are going you will be safe. It is not safe for you to try to return to your lodgings tonight; Estaban said there were nearly a dozen of them. They will be watching everywhere and they must not see you during the dark hours."

Slade had his own opinion relative to that and was not particularly perturbed over a prospect of another brush with the killers, especially in the open, but he decided to go along with her. Partly out of curiosity, partly because he considered it would be ungrateful not to fall in with her wishes after all she'd done for him.

"Okay," he said, "but I really don't think it's necessary to go up the ramp and across the bridge at a run. Also it might attract unfavorable attention at the toll booth."

"You are right," she agreed. "And it is safe to walk now."

"I can't help but he bothered about Estaban," Slade observed. "I don't feel right about leaving him alone back there."

"Don't worry about him," she returned. "He is quick and cunning as the Indians among whom he was reared. I hope those *ladrones* follow him. If so, he will lead them into an ambush from which not one will escape alive."

Before they were halfway across the bridge, Slade noticed that her steps were faltering a trifle.

"It is nothing," she said, "only we did run fast and far."

Slade laughed; reaching down, he picked her up lightly and cradled her in his arms.

"Better?" he asked.

"Much," she replied, "but you—you also must be exhausted."

"Oh, I've caught my second wind," he replied cheerfully. "I'm set to do it all over again if necessary."

"You are very strong," she said, nestling closer.

"You're not very heavy," he countered. "No bigger'n a minute."

"I'm big enough."

"I don't doubt it," he chuckled, tightening his arms a bit. Even in the moonlight which was not dappling the water of the Rio Grande with silver he could see her blush. The big eyes slanted up to meet his, then the silken curtain of her lashes fluttered down before he could read their expression. Which he regretted.

"Estaban, is he your—*amante?*" he asked.

"No, he is not my sweetheart—I have no sweetheart," she replied. "He is married to my elder sister. They live in Nuevo Laredo."

"And are you from Nuevo Laredo?" She shook her curly head.

"I am Texas born," she answered. "As my father before me, and his father and his father's father."

"One of the old Spanish families, eh?" Slade remarked. He had been wondering about her choice of words. "How come you are dancing in a cantina?" he asked. She shrugged daintily.

"One must live," she said. "Our *hacienda* was taken from us. My father could not produce the old original Spanish grant and without it the court held his title was not valid."

"Did he appeal the decision?" Slade asked. "Often the higher courts have ruled that if the original grants cannot be produced, corroborative evidence of some sort is all that is necessary to secure the title."

"He died very shortly after the court decision," she replied. "He was found dead at the foot of a cliff, from the crest of which he had jumped or fallen."

"Or had possibly been *helped* to fall," Slade commented grimly.

"It could have been so," she conceded.

"I see," Slade said quietly, and suddenly his eyes were the color of snow-sifted winter ice under a cloudy sky.

Again the big eyes slanted up to his face; she shivered a little in his arms.

"What's the matter?" he asked. "Cold?"

"No, I am not cold," she answered. "But when you look like that—I almost fear you."

Abruptly his eyes were filled with the little dancing devils of laughter and he smiled, the flashing white smile of *El Halcon*, that men—and women—found irresistible.

"You need never fear me, little one," he said.

Again her long lashes lowered. "No?" she murmured, her voice suddenly soft and slumberous. "No? When you look like *that*—I fear you even more!"

"Explain."

"I don't think it's necessary," she parried. "I'm not the first woman *El Halcon* has held in his arms. Nor— the last."

"I'm not so sure about that," he answered impulsively.

And it was not just because she had undoubtedly saved his life, just as undoubtedly at the risk of her own. Walt Slade greatly admired courage, and she had proven that she had it, in abundance. There was something very alluring, and disturbing, about this small danced floor girl with the big eyes. He tried to concentrate on the problems that confronted him, and failed signally.

They reached the end of the bridge, and saw people coming up the ramp.

"Really you must put me down now," she said. "There are many rather prim people over here, who very probably would be scandalized."

Slade chuckled, lifted her higher against his breast, and their lips met. Her arms tightened around his neck for a moment, then she laughed gaily and dropped lightly to the ground.

"Say!" he exclaimed. "I don't even know your name."

"It is Marie," she replied. "Marie Telo."

"Telo," he repeated. "That was the name of a very illustrious Spanish family, for centuries the bar on the northern gate of Spain."

"That was long ago," she answered lightly. "This Telo is just a dancing girl in a cantina."

"For whose feet old Don Pedro Calderon Barca de la Telo would doubtless sweep a path with his sombrero," Slade replied.

"You seem to know a great deal about my—about the Telo family," she observed wonderingly.

"Spanish history always interested me," he explained. "I recall famous names and their exploits, and Don Pedro's were many and outstanding."

"The dead past buries its dead, and the rose that blooms today quickly fades," she returned lightly.

"So, 'Gather ye roses while ye may,'" he smilingly quoted.

"While ye may," she repeated.

They had reached the street and strolled along it, arm in arm. Late though it was, there was plenty of activity, for Nuevo Laredo, like its sister town across the river, apparently required little sleep. They passed through the "Meat Market," three blocks south of the bridge, a typical market of Mexico. It covered nearly an entire block and housed venders of meats, fruits and vegetables and exotic foods peculiar to the land of manana. Also displayed were costly jewelry, rare perfumes, less expensive pottery, basketware and garish copies of Aztec art. A gambling wheel near the center of the market was doing a flourishing business. Stray dogs drank contentedly from the overflow of a spring.

On corners, wandering troubadours strummed guitars and sang folk songs of Mexico. For the most part they dressed in charro costumes, including gay sombreros, embroidered serapes and tight-fitting velvet pantaloons adorned with much silver. Always they were the center of a throng that tossed them small coins when they paused for breath.

Turning a corner, Marie Telo paused before a brightly-lighted cantina from which came song and laughter.

"Shall we go in?" she suggested. "Estaban will meet us here."

They entered and found a table near the bar. Marie gazed about her contentedly.

"I like this place," she said. "The people here are always gay. Even those who have little to be gay about seem happy. Gathering roses while they may."

"I sometimes think they have the true wisdom," Slade replied gravely. "Living for the hour and what the hour has to give. And sufficient unto eternity is the glory of the hour."

"Yes," she answered.

Sitting in silence, sipping the wine Slade ordered, they watched the colorful scene. Everybody did seem happy, even peons in ragged serapes and hempen sandals on their feet. Slade also liked the place.

A man entered, a small, slender, elegant man whose movements were singularly graceful. He was greeted by respectful salutations by all who met his gaze. Room was instantly made for him at the bar.

"Who's that?" Slade asked.

"He calls himself *Un Grande de General*, but others have another name for him," Marie replied.

"The other name?"

"*El Cascabell*"

8

WALT SLADE STARED, and his lips pursed in a soundless whistle.

"He is not aptly named," Marie pursued. "The rattle-snake warns before striking. Ralpho Flores never warns, and his stroke is as deadly."

"Flores," Slade repeated.

"Yes, he claims to be a descendant of General Juan Flores of Las Cuevas. Perhaps he is."

There is a sandy road leading from the banks of the river at Rio Grande City through the old town of Camargo down the river through the brush to Las Cuevas. Close to the road stands an imposing inscribed monument more than fifteen feet high, surmounted by a cross, and ofttimes decorated with wreaths of flowers. The inscription, in Spanish, reads:

To Citizen
JUAN FLORES
Who Fighting
Died For His Country

Walt Slade had seen that tribute erected to the man whom many looked upon as a patriot but whom others considered a Border bandit. He regarded the little man at the bar with interest.

Ralpho Flores looked as unlike a notorious bandit leader as any small, apparently inoffensive gentleman possibly could. Then, as Flores turned his head, Slade noted something he had missed before: his eyes seemed to burn. And, which lent credence to his claim of descent, for General Juan Flores had himself been that rarity, a blue-eyed Mexican; Flores' eyes were blue. Those fire-filled eyes instantly set him apart.

And as Slade studied him more closely, he noted something else—they never seemed to blink. They were like unto the lidless eyes of the deadly reptile for which he was named, eternally staring, seeing all things, mir-

53

roring nothing. Ralpho Flores'- eyes would never reveal his thoughts, never signal the move he intended to make. *El Cascabel!* The name *did* fit!

At the bar, several men were talking earnestly to Flores. Twice he turned and gazed in Slade's direction.

"I think they are discussing you, Mr. Slade," Marie said nervously.

"Let them discuss," Slade replied composedly. "Incidentally, my first name happens to be Walt. Suppose you use it. I don't believe in formality between—friends."

A dimple showed at the corner of her red mouth and her eyes slanted toward him in the manner he thought most provocative.

"Very well—Walt," she said. "Good gracious! Flores is coming this way!"

Ralpho Flores had indeed turned from the bar and was walking straight to the table. He halted but a few feet distant, facing Slade.

"*Senor,*" he said in a high voice that was still not unmusical. "*Senor,* you will sing for me."

Slade looked him up and down as if seeing him for the first time.

"Don't recall signing up with you, sir," he drawled.

"What do you mean?" Flores demanded. His eyes did not change, but his face looked puzzled, slightly bewildered, in fact.

"I mean," Slade said quietly, "that I don't take orders from a man unless I happen to be working for him."

Flores' mouth tightened. For a moment the fiery blue eyes and the cold gray locked glances like rapier blades. Then abruptly Flores smiled, a very winning smile, Slade thought, although his eyes did not change.

"*Senor,* your pardon," he said. "When one is accustomed to command, one becomes forgetful. *Will* you sing for me? I would consider it the great favor and an honor. I do love good music, of which I hear so little. I am told that you sing as few can. Please, *senor.*"

"I'll be happy to oblige," Slade replied, rising to his feet and towering over Flores. He turned at a touch on his arm. The smiling orchestra leader was standing to one side, holding a guitar.

"Will *Capitan* not come to the *plataforma?*" he requested.

Slade nodded, accepted the guitar and walked to the little raised dais which accommodated the musicians. A hush fell as he turned to face the expectant crowd. Marie had gestured Flores to the chair he had quitted. The bandit leader sat gazing at Slade, his thin aristocratic-looking hands folded before him.

Tuning the guitar to his liking, Slade played a soft prelude. Then he flung back his black head and sang, sang in Spanish a simple but heart-warming song of *Mejico*, a song that the peons loved. And as the golden baritone-bass soared and lilted, drinks and cards and the dance were forgotten. Ralpho Flores sat with his gaze fixed on the singer and the hard lines of his face had softened and even the fire in his eyes seemed to have lost some of its intensity.

The music ended with a crash of chords and was followed by a storm of *vivas!* and shouts of "*Otro! Otro!*"—another!

Slade sang them another, two more, in fact, a rollicking ballad of the range and a dreamy love song of old Spain. Returning the guitar to its owner, he walked back to the table.

Ralpho Flores started, as one does from a dream. For a long moment he regarded Slade in silence. Then he slowly rose to his feet, his small form lance-straight.

"*Gracias, senor! gracias!*" he said. "Truly, I thank you!" He turned on his heel and walked out into the night.

"A strange man," Slade observed. "On the right trail he could go far."

Marie was gazing at him, an expression in her beautiful eyes that was not hard to read.

"Walt," she said slowly, "I think you made a friend."

Slade laughed. After all, there was a certain element of humor in the situation. A Texas Ranger singing for a bandit leader and making a friend of him! Well, to such base uses do we come!

Estaban sauntered in. He sat down, his black eyes twinkling.

"So! Another conquest, eh?" he remarked, pouring himself a glass of wine. "I was standing just outside the door, listening. *El Cascabel* came out and didn't even notice me. He looked as if he had just seen a vision.

Music is his weakness, as everybody knows. *Senor*, it would seem you charmed the serpent."

Slade laughed again. "But serpents don't stay charmed," he pointed out.

"All you need to do to charm Ralpho Flores is sing to him," Estaban replied. "If you'd just sung to those *ladrones* across the river, they'd have dropped their guns and shed tears. Not that they didn't shed tears anyhow, several of them."

"I didn't think it wise to try the experiment," Slade answered.

Estaban tossed off his glass and twinkled his eyes at Marie.

"Little one," he said, "either you dream or you are sleepy. Come, the dawn draws near and I hate to see the sunrise. Come, *senor*, it is time to rest."

Through the rose and gold glory of the morning, Estaban led them to a neat little two-storied house on a quiet side street. When he opened the door, a woman rose from a chair to greet them.

"Rosa," said Marie, "this is Walt Slade—*El Halcon*. Walt, my sister, Rosa Fuentes."

Rosa Fuentes was much taller than her sister, but she had the same slender, graceful figure and the same beautiful dark eyes. Eyes that always seemed filled with laughter. She extended a little sun-golden hand over which Slade bowed with courtly grace.

"Gracious!" she exclaimed. "How tall you are! And such shoulders! Marie would look like a doll in your arms!"

"How do you know I was in his arms?" Marie demanded, blushing hotly. Rosa's eyes were all innocence.

"I didn't know, small sister, until you just told me," she replied. "Well, who can blame you. But, come, it is time to rest. This husband of mine! He is one with the owls. Never does he see the sunrise, but he always sees it set."

She led Slade up the stairs to an immaculate little room under the eaves. Suddenly her eyes danced.

"If you wish anything, just call," she said. "Marie sleeps right across the hall. Assuredly she will hear and heed."

She motioned to a door that stood slightly ajar and with a little trill of laughter was gone. Slade closed his door, sat down in a chair by the window and rolled a cigarette. It appeared things were getting more complicated by the minute, but not unpleasantly. In the hall outside, he heard Marie's light step as she entered her room. A little later he pinched out the cigarette, gazed at the closed door for a moment, and drew the shade.

It was well past noon and sunlight was filtering through the window shade when Slade awakened. For a while he lay thinking over the happenings of the night before. They had been very hectic, but not altogether without value. He had learned that he was up against an utterly ruthless and well-organized outfit that would stop at nothing. However, with the help of Estaban and Marie, the bunch had been taught a lesson they were not likely to soon forget. There was some comfort to be gleaned from that fact, although he knew well he had only scotched the snake, not killed it. Cale Brandon was still running around loose and so long as Brandon was active, he could expect more trouble. Also, he wondered, was there somewhere in the background a smarter man than Brandon who pulled the wires. Slade had learned that often the front man and apparent leader of such an outfit was really but a "hired hand" whose moves were directed by the real mastermind who was not in evidence, for a while, anyhow.

But in this particular case, who the devil could be the mastermind, if not Brandon? Well, he was new to the section and not yet in a position to judge.

His thoughts turned to Ralpho Flores. There was a man of undoubted ability. Could he possibly be the moving force behind the mysterious project which involved the acquiring of the farm lands of the valley. Slade hardly thought so, but it was possible. Flores must not be immediately rejected. If such a thing were true, he had a feeling that sooner or later Flores would approach him as a possible ally. The man's undoubted love of music might be the key which would unlock the mystery. That is, if Flores really was concerned. Well, as to that, time would tell. He dressed and went downstairs to the living room where he found the two girls awaiting him. Rosa was all laughter, Marie all blushes when he appeared.

"We waited to eat with you," said Rosa. "Estaban has gone to work."

"He couldn't have had much sleep," Slade commented.

"Oh, he sleeps well in the saddle," Rosa replied. "He'll catch a few winks while he's riding."

"He's a vaquero?" Slade asked.

"He was," said Rosa. "Now he is a major-domo of the great Garcia *hacienda*, and old Manuel Garcia's right-hand man. A range boss, we would say in Texas."

"More in the nature of a manager, I'd say," Slade observed.

"Yes," Rosa answered. "Come along, I'm hungry. Marie is always hungry, and you must be starved."

It was a very jolly breakfast, eaten with the appetite of youth and perfect health. After smoking a cigarette, Slade drew a notebook and a pencil from his pocket.

"Rosa," he said, "I want you and Marie to tell me everything you can about your father's ranch that was taken from him. All you can about the Spanish grant he could not produce, and any corroborative evidence that the grant was issued. I want the name of the ranch, the registered brand, the number of years, as near as you can recall, that the land was owned and occupied by your family, and anything else you can think of. Also, who brought the suit that was decided against your father in the lower court, and the name of the lawyer who handled the case, if you remember."

The two girls complied. Slade carefully jotted down all the answers, and as he did so, his eyes grew colder.

"You're sure about the lawyer's name?" he said.

"Yes, we are sure," Rosa replied.

Slade snapped up the notebook, the contents of which would be incorporated in a letter he would write without delay and send to Captain McNelty as ranger post headquarters.

"I don't think you'll need to dance in a cantina much longer," he told Marie. "For a couple of reasons."

Marie smiled, and did not question him.

Slade was dubious about her going to work in the cantina that night, but she stilled his objections.

"There is nothing to fear," she said. "I have many friends there, including the owner, who was my father's friend. And even were it not so, who would dare injure the—friend—of *El Halcon?*"

They walked across the bridge together in the glow of twilight. Slade left her at the door of the cantina.

"I'll be seeing you soon," he promised.

"And take care of yourself," she begged. "You must!"

9

SLADE DROPPED IN at the sheriff's and found Tobe Medford at his desk.

"Well!" exclaimed the peace officer. "Where have you been? I was beginning to think you'd show up among the missing. There was one devil of a row last night in a cantina down on Grant Street; the place was a wreck. Two dead men by the front door. Another one in the alley back of the place, his throat slashed. Another shooting over toward the bridge, but we didn't find any bodies there. Of course nobody saw anything, as usual. All we could learn was that there was a row started by somebody and then somebody shot out the lights. You can never induce anybody to talk in those places by the river. All right, what did happen? I know darn well you were in the middle of it."

Slade told him, in detail. The sheriff listened with absorbed interest.

"That little Telo gal is okay," he said when Slade paused. "I know her. Knew her dad, too, Sebastian Telo. Real *hidalgo* stock. Sebastian Telo was one of the old Dons from a different age. A real gentleman who trusted everybody and knew nothing of the ins and outs of the law business. After he lost the spread and fell over a cliff and killed himself, the gal refused to allow her brother-in-law Estaben Fuentes to support her, which he was willing and glad to do, and went to work in the cantina. Yes, she's okay, and so is Estaban. I'd have liked to see him pitch that knife. He's a wonder at it, I've been told."

"Funny how things work around," Slade said musingly. "The Telo land case may develop into the crux of the situation. I'm convinced it was a downright fraud, with perhaps perjured testimony. I intend to get to the bottom of it. I was surprised to learn that Wilton Danver handled the case of the Land Committee."

'He's a lawyer and works both sides of the street," replied the sheriff. "He won a case against the Land Com-

60

mittee, too. The case of Pablo Navarez, who owns a spread over to the east where the hills begin. Navarez couldn't produce his grant, either, but Danver dug up a bunch of old promissory notes signed by Laredo folks for money lent them by Pablo's grandfather, and each and every one of them made mention of the old Spanish grant by which Pablo held his land. Danver won his case hands down. The Land Committee did a lot of cussin', but it didn't do 'em any good. They didn't even appeal."

"I see," Slade said thoughtfully. He made a mental note to learn more about the Pablo Navarez case.

"Anyhow, it appears you've got a tough bunch after you," observed the sheriff.

"Yes, it looks sort of that way," Slade conceded. "And I still don't know why they want that land. Also, I have no proof that the Land Commmittee had anything to do with what happened last night. And not the slightest idea why somebody wanted to kill Wilton Danver. Well, at least they're being thinned out a bit."

"That helps some," agreed the sheriff. "Well, let's go over to The Montezuma and eat. I figure you'll be reasonably safe there and maybe we can think of something."

"I hope so," Slade said. "It's a mess."

"Oh, you'll get to the bottom of it, sooner or later," the sheriff predicted cheerfully. "That is, if you manage to stay alive long enough."

"I'm still kicking, and that's what counts," Slade smiled. "Let's go."

"What do you think of *El Cascabel?*" Medford asked as they crossed the street.

"He's a puzzler," Slade answered. "I don't know for sure just what to think of him. At first look, you'd think he was a store clerk or something of the sort. Then take a good look and you quickly decide he's not."

"Calls himself a liberator, and a lot of folks on both sides of the river figure he is," said Medford. "Seems to have a stand-in with the governor of the state and other officials over there, although I understand old *Presidente* Diaz has put a price on his head. No doubt but he's done a lot of cow stealing and such, but they've got notions about such things in *manana* land, especially if the stealing is done in Texas."

"Down there it's hard to tell what is a liberator and what is a *bandido*," Slade said. "He looks to be either, or both."

"Wouldn't be surprised if that's about the size of it," nodded Medford.

"Wonder if he has any connections on this side of the river?"

"That's another one hard to answer," said Medford. "I sometimes think maybe he has. Can't tell, though. He comes and goes as he pleases in Nuevo Laredo, but he stays away from Laredo, so far as anybody seems to know. May slip over in disguise, though."

"He'd have to be blindfolded to disguise those eyes," Slade declared with conviction. "They're unique. Well, here we are. Let's eat."

Laredo was not the only center of activity in the Rio Grande Valley. Old Felipe Cardena sat by his fireside pondering the word that shortly before had been brought him by a messenger who slipped in the back way. He smoked a husk cigarette in leisurely fashion and with evident enjoyment. Suddenly he cocked his head in an attitude of listening. He turned slightly toward a door to the left of the front door, which led into a dark inner room, and nodded. He did not appear at all surprised when the front door slammed open and half a dozen men bulged into the room. Their hatbrims were pulled low, their neckerchiefs muffled up almost to their eyes.

"All right, Cardena," one said gutterally, "we've come for you. You're going with us."

"Certainly, *senores*," Felipe replied courteously, "but first would the *senores* please to look to the left?"

Eyes slanted toward the door of the back room. The raiders stiffened. They were looking into the muzzles of six leveled rifles. Behind the muzzles were glittering black eyes, and dark, grim faces.

"Have the care, *senores*," said Felipe, still courteous. "My *amigos* have the trigger fingers that itch. You will please to turn to the wall and raise your hands against it— high."

Cursing and fuming, the raiders obeyed. Felipe, taking care to keep out of line with the rifle muzzles, sauntered over and relieved them of their hardware, which he piled on a table out of reach.

"Keep them covered, amigos," he told the riflemen, and strolled out the front door. In a few minutes he returned with an armload of rifles, which he placed beside the six-guns.

"Now, senores, you may turn," he said. "And please to remove the masks."

The raiders hesitated, but the double cock of an uncocked and cocked rifle decided them. The hatbrims were pushed up, the neckerchiefs pulled down, revealing hard, anger-distorted faces.

"So," said Felipe, "ladrones of the brush. But the Senor Brandon is not here, which is a pity. It would be well that he were here, to also remain here."

The old man's voice had taken on a steely edge. The raiders whitened.

"You—you ain't going to murder us!" one mouthed thickly.

"Why not?" asked Felipe. "You came to murder me."

"We—we weren't going to do anything to you," the other stuttered. "We just wanted to talk to you."

"Los muertos no hablan," murmured Felipe.

The other evidently knew enough Spanish to translate—"The dead do not talk." He shivered.

One of the riflemen spoke. "When you give the word, Felipe. We are ready."

The terrified raiders cowered against the wall. One let out a dismal howl. The others gabbled incoherent supplications. Felipe slowly raised his hand. Then he dropped it.

"Ladrones," he said, "we are not going to kill you—now. We do not kill in blood that is cold. Go back to the Senor Brandon and tell him that we of the valley no longer fear him. There is one here now who banishes fear. Tell him to beware. To beware the vengeance of El Halcon! Go!"

They went, nor did they hesitate on the order of their going.

From the inner room came a disappointed wail. "Please, Felipe," called a voice. "May we not kill just one? One would never be missed."

With a strangled squawk of sheer panic, the last raider

scuttled out the door like a scared rat. Felipe smilingly shook his head.

"No," he said. "Then we would have to bury him, and that is labor."

Outside, frantic hoofs drummed away into the distance.

The Texas-Mexican riflemen filed from the inner room, chuckling. "That was well done, Felipe, you played that pipe well," said one. "You frightened those *ladrones*, and they will frighten their master. Ha! Wise are the words of *El Halcon*, who said those whose cause is just need never fear."

"Wise, too, when he warned me to be prepared for just what happened tonight. Aye! *El Halcon* is wise, and the wise heed his words. We will remain ever vigilant, and fear not at all."

10

THE POKER GAME at the big table by the window was in full swing when Slade and the sheriff entered The Montezuma. Cale Brandon was one of the players, Wilton Danver another. Shortly after they sat down and ordered a meal, Wilton Danver left the poker game and approached their table. Sheriff Medford waved him to a chair.

He sat down and said, "Mr. Slade—I believe that's your name, and doubtless you know mine. I was in somewhat of a state of shock the other night and failed to adequately thank you for what you did in my behalf. I wish to make up for that neglect; you undoubtedly saved my life, and I am truly grateful. If at any time I can do you a favor, no matter what, please don't hesitate to ask."

"Thank you, Mr. Danver," Slade replied. "What I did was in the nature of obeying an impulse, without thinking."

"I'm glad you didn't take time to think before acting," Danver said, with a wry smile. "Otherwise I doubt if I would be here talking to you right now. It isn't easy to express my appreciation in words, but perhaps the time will come when I can do so more appropriately. Do you plan to remain with us?"

"For a while, possibly, if I happen to tie onto something to my liking," Slade evaded.

"I'll speak to some of my rancher friends in your behalf," Danver promised. "I feel pretty sure they'd be glad to have such a tophand, as you undoubtedly are, sign up with them."

With a smile and a nod, he rose to his feet and returned to the game. Cale Brandon growled something to him as he sat down, but did not deign to glance in Slade's direction.

"A nice feller, Danver, and I've a notion he meant what he said," commented the sheriff.

"Yes, he appears to be," Slade conceded, "but if he was in a state of shock the other night, as he claimed to be, I wouldn't want to meet a mountain lion or a grizzly in the same condition. He was ready to shoot it out with all and sundry if he could just figure whom to shoot at. He never turned a hair and went back to his cards as if nothing had happened. Most anyone would have moved his chair to another position, but Danver sat on right where he was."

"That sort of points to plenty of guts," observed the sheriff.

"Rather, to plenty of savvy and a quick sizing up of the situation," Slade differed. "He knew very well that a second try wouldn't be made that night and reacted accordingly. You'll notice that tonight he has the window to the side of him, where he can keep an eye on it without seeming to do so. He's a cool customer, all right, with no nerves at all. No wonder he's doing well in his law business; the sort that misses no details and anticipates the move the other fellow is going to make well before it's made. Or at least that's the opinion I've formed of him."

"Wouldn't argue with you for a minute," said the sheriff. "And I've a notion he doesn't put much stock in El Halcon yarns that are going around."

"More likely he doesn't give a darn," Slade answered. "As you said, he's a lawyer and works both sides of the street, as most successful lawyers do. All's grist to his mill. He probably thinks that defending El Halcon in court in case he slips up in some of his activities and falls foul of the law might be lucrative. An eye for business."

"Wouldn't be surprised," conceded Medford, with a chuckle. "I've got a notion, too, that he put a bug in Cale Brandon's ear and told him to lay off you. Brandon hasn't been sounding off to me since the night you saved Danver from getting plugged. I figure Danver packs considerable influence with the horned toad."

Slade nodded agreement. It was not improbable that Danver, as his legal adviser, had warned Brandon that making big medicine about what he couldn't prove, might work to his disadvantage.

"Brandon's a blowhard, but don't underestimate him," warned Medford. "He's the sort that bides his time and waits until he's got you at a disadvantage. Wouldn't be surprised if he figures that sooner or later you'll make a little slip and then he'll help the law crack down on you."

"I hope that's what he's got in mind, but I don't think it is," Slade replied. "I think he's waiting for an opportunity to personally even up the score, and if he gets the chance he won't ask the law to help."

"You may be right," admitted Medford. "Anyhow, watch him. I'm doing just that, and I've a feeling that sooner or later I'll get a chance to drop a loop on the sidewinder. So far he's always managed to stay inside the law, so far as anybody's been able to prove. But what he did to Felipe Cardena was very much outside the law, and if he'll do it one time he'll do it another, if he figures he can get by with it."

Slade nodded agreement, pushed back his empty plate and rolled a cigarette.

"I'm going to bed," he announced. "Had very little sleep for the past couple of nights and I'm beginning to feel it. Figure to take a little ride tomorrow.'

"Okay, but watch your step," said the sheriff. "As I said before, there's no doubt that you've got a bad bunch riding herd on you. Watch your step."

Early morning next day found Slade in the saddle and riding east at a leisurely pace. He passed many little homes, each with its garden and patch of cultivated land. Also some very small spreads where cattle grazed. There was a smile on his lips as he watched the humble dwellers of the valley going about their various chores, but his eyes grew cold as he thought on that which he felt sure was a callous plot to rob them of their small holdings. The puzzler, however, was why? For the life of him he couldn't see why anybody would go to such lengths to secure the unprofitable land. It was fit only for what it was being used, to provide a scanty living for those willing to work hard and expect little. Any practicable method of increasing its value would require a great outlay of capital. There was one possible method he considered, but that appeared out of the question. It certainly was so far as the present inhabitants of the valley were concerned. Of course, not all of the land was privately owned; much of it was state land and amenable to purchase, or had been. He did not know whether the Land Committee had tied onto it, or if possibly someone else had.

He rode on, pondering the problem but always with close-attention to his surroundings. He did not really expect any trouble here in the open land, especially with Shadow between his thighs. The big horse could show a clean pair of heels to anything that attempted to overtake him and here it was not possible to either ambush or surround him. Just the same, Slade took no chances. He carefully watched the actions of birds on the wing, of little animals, studied each thicket, analyzed drifting shadows.

He had ridden quite a few miles over the flat expanse that was but little above the water level of the Rio Grande. Then the terrain began to change slightly, sloping upward from the river to quickly reach a considerable height beyond that of the riverbed, and became somewhat rolling in contour, with occasional small, low hills that increased in height and frequency to the north. Here he began to see cows wearing a Lazy P brand, which he knew to be the burn of Pablo Navarez, whose spread Wilton Danver had rescued from the clutches of the Land Committee. He pulled up and studied the topographical features.

"Higher, more rugged, but with better grass than back there to the west," he told Shadow. "Not bad for cows, but would be poor for even small farming. Reckon that's why the Texas-Mexicans and others never spread this way. Nothing much to be learned here, so far as I can see, but, horse, I somehow have a feeling that there is something, if I can just figure it out. Also, we're going to keep on going until we strike the railhead of the new railroad headed this way. There are the stakes marking their survey line, right ahead. Another ten miles and we should do it. Right through here is where the line will come. Maybe we can learn something of value there."

Shadow snorted cheerful agreement and ambled on at a good pace, veering somewhat to the north. Slade noted that the terrain was not at all bad for road building, with no major obstructions.

The sun was well up toward the zenith when he saw smoke shifting against the sky.

"That's a construction train moving ahead," he told Shadow. "Clear that front pitch of brush and we should see it."

Slade's estimate was correct. A litle later he saw the

crawling worm that was the train. He rode on until he reached a scene of activity. Ties were being unloaded, and rails. Mauls thudded as they were spiked in place ahead of the train. Nearer to where he rode, grading was in progress. He rode on until he reached the point where the pick and shovel men were hard at work. Sauntering about was a pleasant but rather pompous-looking individual that Slade decided was the engineer in charge. He rode on slowly.

The engineer waved his hand. "Howdy, cowboy?" he called. "Here we come with the iron horse that will make your horse obsolete."

"I doubt it," Slade smiled reply, "but it will give him some competition, perhaps render him obsolescent before so very long."

The engineer looked a bit surprised at him using the word with its slightly different meaning from "obsolete." Slade decided to puzzle him a bit more. He asked a few casual questions that caused the other to open his eyes.

"It would appear you know something about this business," he commented.

"I've worked with surveying gangs a few times, in off-seasons," Slade explained. He did not mention in what capacity.

"Then you'll appreciate what we are doing," the engineer said.

Slade nodded. "Anyhow you have a terrain which offers few difficulties," he remarked.

"Yes," said the engineer, "all easy going." He studied Slade a moment. "Except for a tunnel we'll have to run about five miles farther on, when we're getting closer to the river."

"A tunnel?"

"Uh-huh, through a hill that stands right in our survey line. We'll have to run a five-hundred-foot tunnel through it. Here, I'll show you."

He took a roll from a knapsack he carried and spread it out.

"See?" he said, dabbing a finger at a spot. "T for tunnel."

"I see," Slade nodded. He glanced over the survey plat, which was covered with tiny-lettered notations in engineering jargon.

"What are all these lines farther on that look to run to the river?" he asked.

"Oh, those will be feeders leading to the big assembly yards that will be built nearer the river," the engineer explained airily. "Junction yards. There's another road building up from Mexico City, you know. It'll reach Laredo a year or so after we do. And this line won't stop at Laredo; it'll go right on to the west coast."

Slade nodded. "Going to give the S.P. and the T. & P. some competition, eh?"

"That's right," the engineer replied complacently. "We'll make 'em hump themselves."

Slade watched the construction work for a little while, then gathered up the reins.

"Have to be getting back on the job," he told the engineer. "Saw your smoke and took a notion to ride over and see how things were going."

"Come around any time you take a notion," invited the engineer. Slade waved his hand and rode back the way he had come. The engineer turned to his transit man, a leathery-faced individual with keen eyes, who stood within hearing distance.

"Wonder who he is and what did he want here?" he remarked. The transit man gazed after the retreating horseman and shook his head.

"Well, if he was trying to find out something about things not supposed to be generally known, I threw him off," said the engineer. "He knows something about surveying, but not much. Yep, I threw him off. Don't you think so?"

"No, I don't," the transit man replied flatly. "Why did you hand him that guff about the tunnel?"

"I wanted to see if he'd swallow it; he did. Don't you think so?"

"No, I don't," the transit man said, just as flatly.

"What do you mean?" the engineer demanded belligerently.

"I mean you didn't fool him one bit with that nonsense," said the transit man. "All you did was start him to wondering why you tried to feed him such a yarn. Listen, Al, I'm not an engineer and a college graduate like you are, but I've been around a lot and I know men. That young feller is one of the most remarkable characters

I ever laid eyes on. He'd stand out in any crowd like a mahogany stake in a line of pine ones. Did you happen to pay attention to his eyes?"

"No, I didn't," the other answered. "Why?"

"Because," the transit man said slowly, "they are the kind of eyes that look right inside you and see what's there. And if there are any dark places, or things you don't want known about you, look out! You didn't fool him one bit with your line, and if he wants to find out something, he'll find out. Mark what I tell you."

The engineer grew decidedly irritated. "I've known you to make some very serious mistakes," he snapped.

"Then why do you ask my advice about things?"

The engineer swore. "Blast it! You've got me worried," he concluded. "If there's a leak and it's traced to me, I'm in trouble."

"It'll never be traced to you through that young feller," the transit man stated positively.

"Why not?"

"Because he's not the sort to make trouble for a hired hand. And if he's really after something, it's big game, not small fry like you and me. Of course he may not have had anything in mind, just curious. Anyhow, I sure wouldn't want him on my trail for any reason."

"What do you think he is?"

"I don't know what else," said the transit man, "but I'm willing to bet a hatful of pesos that he's one of the best engineers that ever rode across Texas. You didn't notice how his eyes went over that plat when you showed it to him, but I did. They took in everything on it in a glance, and understood everything on it. That's the only time his face changed a bit. All of a sudden that furrow between his brows deepened, which was a sign that he was doing some fast thinking or I miss my guess. Right now he's trying to figure what those lines leading to the river really do mean, and he'll get the right answer, too, if he really has a reason for getting it.'

All of which showed the transit man was not bad at reading character.

11

SLADE RODE STEADILY until, some miles farther to the west, he approached a small, very sharp-pointed peak around which the line of survey stakes curved. He pulled up and sat regarding it.

"That's it, Shadow," he said. "That's the hill our *amigo* back there said he's going to tunnel. Well, if he runs a five-hundred-foot tunnel through that hill it will be one of the most expensive and arduous undertakings that was ever conceived by man. It is not more than two hundred feet through from side to side; which means he'll have to build three hundred feet of his tunnel on trestle-work!"

"And 'T' for tunnel! That 'T' stands for 'topographical obstruction.' What he was talking to me was gibberish. Scientific gibberish!

"And that plat! It is a topographic survey of the valley between the Pablo Navarez ranch and Laredo, complete with surface contours, elevations, hachures, and showing soil conditions in meticulous detail, and taking the mean level of the Rio Grande River as a base-line. What in blazes was that jigger trying to do? Going to the trouble to hand me a lot of sheep dip that way! Looks like he was trying hard to cover up something and doing it clumsily. Waited a moment after speaking of tunneling that hill, as if to see how I'd take it."

Shadow apparently couldn't answer, or wouldn't answer the question. Slade hooked one long leg over the saddle horn, rolled a cigarette with the slim fingers of his left hand and smoked in leisurely comfort, the concentration furrow deep between his black brows. Which the transit man would have more than ever been convinced was a sign of hard thinking; in which he would have been right.

"Feller," Slade said as he pinched out the butt and settled himself in the saddle, "feller, I don't know for sure what it's all about, but I'm getting a notion. Yes, I'm getting a notion. But if I'm right, why in blazes did that blasted Land Committee try hard to tie onto the Pablo Navarez holding, which would certainly be of no value to them! Well, it's up to us to find the answers. Feller, you've got a hard jaunt ahead of you, but we've got to gather some corroborative information, if possible, to bolster my hunch. Into the brush and up the slope with you!"

Shadow snorted his disgust but obediently breasted the brush covered slope, which really was not a particularly difficult undertaking for a horse of his strength and agility.

Slade knew that some forty miles to the north was a railroad telegraph station which had an operator on duty all night. For that station he headed.

All the long afternoon he rode steadily, allowing Shadow to drink from some stream now and then and crop a little grass. The sun sank in flaming splendor. The twilight deepened. Birds uttered their sleepy calls. The stars bloomed in the sky, casting a faint and silvery sheen over the rolling prairie. And still the great black horse forged tirelessly on. Slade talked and joked with him, promising him a hefty helping of oats when the chore was finished. Shadow took it all in good part and never faltered.

The night was pretty well on when Slade saw, some distance ahead, a wide straggling of lights that he knew must be the little village which was his destination. The wail of a whistle, still thin with distance, broke the silence. A little later, a long freight train roared past a few hundred yards to the front, locomotive exhaust pounding, side rods clanging. The air was heavy with the pungent whiff of coal smoke, the acrid tang of burned oil and creosote and the cloying odor of crushed fruit. The caboose taillights whisked out of sight around a curve. Slade turned Shadow to the left along the right-of-way and shortly afterward pulled up before the little station. Leaving Shadow tied securely to the night wind, he entered. The operator looked up from his table and waved a greeting.

"Come in out of the cold, cowboy," he invited. "What can I do for you?"

"I'd like to send a message," Slade replied.

The operator hesitated, gazing doubtfully at El Halcon's towering form.

"This is a railroad telegraph—" he began.

Slade slipped something from a cunningly concealed pocket in his broad leather belt and laid it on the table. The operator stared at the famous silver star set on a silver circle, and reached for a blank.

"Okay, Ranger," he said, "let's have it."

"Thank you," Slade said and wrote a terse message directed to Captain McNelty. It read:

Find out who backs building railroad from Corpus Christi to Laredo. Other activities engaged in.

"Tag it 'urgent' and it will be delivered to Captain Jim at once," he told the operator. "You should have an answer in a few hours."

The operator nodded and opened his key. The message clattered over the wires. He closed the key and looked up.

"Any place hereabouts where my horse and I can put on the feed bag while we're awaiting the reply?" Slade asked.

The operator was a jovial soul who evidently welcomed company to relieve the tedium of his lonely vigil.

"I've got a pot of coffee on the boil and a hefty lot of sandwiches and other chuck," he said. "Would be plumb pleased if you'd share with me."

"And I'll be plumb pleased to accept," Slade smiled.

"Fine!" said the operator, hopping up from his chair. "You can put your cavuse under the lean-to in back with my bronk. Bin full of oats. Fill him up plenty. I'd take care of it for you, only I can't leave the key unattended."

Slade made sure all of Shadow's needs were provided for and returned to the office. The operator had already set out the viands and cups of steaming coffee. He waved Slade to a chair.

"Gets sort of lonesome here during the night hours," he said. "Nothing much to do most of the time except to check what passes with the next block tower. Glad to have somebody to talk to."

The operator proved to be a good talker and full of interesting and sometimes mirthful anecdotes and he had a receptive listener. The hours passed swiftly and it was nearly morning when a reply came from Captain McNelty.

Doesn't show on surface. Holding company is big eastern syndicate. Specializes in land reclamation and development. Has bought up all available state land in section. Will gather more details quickly as possible.

Slade read the message twice. Then with its contents clearly cut on the tablets of his mind, he tore the paper to bits and tossed them into the stove. He let the full force of his steady gray eyes rest on the operator's face.

"I know," he said, "that the rules of your company forbid divulgence of the contents of any message that goes over your wires. On this occasion, make very sure that rule is strictly enforced."

"Don't worry, it will be," the operator assured him.

"And I'd take it as a personal favor if you'd forget all about sending the message," Slade added.

The operator stared at him with a puzzled expression. "What message?" he asked. "I don't remember sending any message tonight. You must be imagining things."

They chuckled together. The operator poured more coffee.

"You must be about ready for a mite of shuteye," he observed. "My relief will be here in another hour, and if you're of a mind to, I'll take you to the boardinghouse where I pound my ear along with some of the railroad boys from the maintenance gang. You can get breakfast there, too. The Widow Paisley runs the joint and she sets a good table, as you can figure from the snack she put up for me to take to work."

"If that was a snack, I'm afraid I won't be able to do justice to a full meal on her table," Slade smiled.

"Oh, she likes to see a man eat," the operator chuckled. "She says that was the only thing wrong with her fifth husband—he couldn't eat like the other four. My notion is that they all five foundered trying to pack away what she put before them. She's okay, though, all wool and a yard wide, and that's just what I mean, a yard wide. You can't help but like her."

A little over an hour later, Slade set out with the garrulous operator for the roominghouse. The Widow Paisley proved to be plump and jolly, not so very old and more than passably good-looking. She welcomed Slade, insisted that he eat breakfast before going to bed.

"A man of your inches should always be eating," she declared. "That skinny runt Tommy," she gestured to the operator, "he's the one man I've met I couldn't fill up. Guess that's why I like him. I'll go out and get another plate of eggs."

"Number six!" Slade remarked pointedly to the operator.

"Oh, Lord!" groaned the other, but he didn't look particularly displeased at the possible prospect.

Slade slept soundly in a good bed until early afternoon. When he descended the stairs the Widow Paisley was waiting for him.

"Come along," she said. "Your snack's on the table. The railroad boys are working and won't be in till later. Yes, I'll tell Tommy you asked for him; he never wakes up till sundown. I hope you'll ride this way again soon; you eat like a man should."

Fully fed and in a fairly contented frame of mind, Slade rode south through the golden sunshine of approaching evening. He communed with Shadow who appeared to be in a receptive mood.

"Yes, horse, I believe things are beginning to tie up," he told the cayuse. "I'm not just sure what's in the wind, but I've got a notion. Although I haven't any proof, I at least have an idea why that blasted Land Committee, as they call themselves, want the land and are willing to go to any lengths to tie onto it. No, I'm not sure, but I've got an idea. If that terrapin-brained engineer hadn't been so anxious to cover up, I might not have caught on; showing me that plat was a bad mistake on his part.Well, we'll see; we'll do some digging and maybe we'll strike paydirt."

Shadow snorted.

"Don't be such a pessimist," Slade chided. "But," he continued, "if my hunch is a straight one, why in blazes did the Land Committee try to acquire the Pablo Navarez holding? That land would certainly not be affected advantageously by the project I believe is in the making. Not at its elevation. Well, we'll try to find out about that one, too." He glanced at the westering sun. "Anyhow, it looks like it's going to be another fine night, which helps," he added.

The day before had been a hard one on Shadow, so Slade rode at a leisurely pace. The sun was shouldering the stars aside when he finally reached Laredo and man and horse were both weary. He hesitated a moment, then rode straight across the bridge to Nuevo Laredo. He found suitable accommodations for Shadow and then headed for the home of Estaban Fuentes.

Rosa Fuentes answered his knock. She placed one rosy fingertip to her red lips.

"Marie is asleep," she said. "She always sleeps late before her night off, which is tonight. You look as if you had been up all night, too."

"Been riding all night," Slade admitted.

"I'll make you some breakfast and then you go to bed, too," Rosa said. "Sleep as long as you want to. You and Marie can have a second breakfast together, after you— wake up!" she added with a giggle and skipped away to the kitchen.

12

Slade and Marie did have the second breakfast together, near sunset, and Rosa joined them. While they were still eating, Estaban arrived, hungry but cheerful.

"Was hoping you'd show up," he told Slade. "We'll go to one of the cantinas tonight. Maybe you'll sing for us," he insinuated. "Rosa will love to hear you."

"As sang the Heavenly host!" exclaimed Marie, clasping her hands.

"Yes," said Estaban, suddenly grave. "And they too sang of peace and good will; here we can use both."

They sat with Estaban while he ate. Finally he pushed back his empty plate and rolled a cigarette.

"Ralpho Flores is in town again today," he remarked, gazing out the window.

Slade waited expectantly; he knew more was coming.

"Yes, he is in town today," Estaban repeated. "He talks with many people."

"What does he talk about?" Slade asked.

"He says," Estaban replied slowly, "that the people of our blood north of the river are suffering grievous wrong."

"They have been," Slade conceded.

"He says," continued Estaban, "that it is only the beginning. That all are to be driven from their homes. He says it is not to be tolerated."

"I don't think they will be," Slade said.

"Nor do I, now that *El Halcon* is here," nodded Estaban. "But many people believe him and are incensed. Flores has a persuasive tongue. Also he is a man of action, as we all know, and a leader of men."

"Meaning?" Slade asked.

"Meaning that it is not improbable that trouble of some sort is in the making," said Estaban. "Something which will profit Flores, of course. He always profits from anything he undertakes. He says, of course, that any move he might make will be in answer to a cry for help from the valley dwellers."

78

"Intimating that the move would really be instigated by the valley dwellers, eh?"

"Yes."

"Doesn't he realize that any such thing would crystallize public opinion against the valley dwellers, which at present is veering to their side?"

Estaban shrugged with Latin expressiveness. "*El Cascabel is El Cascabel*," he replied. "What cares he as to the final result, just so *El Cascabel* profits? And it is whispered that there are those north of the river who are friendly to his plans and will lend him aid. Not of Mexican blood."

The concentration furrow deepened between Slade's black brows. "I see," he said quietly. "Thanks for the information, Estaban, it may prove valuable."

"So I thought," said Estaban. "*Si*, I thought that *El Halcon* should know."

"Knowledge learned is power earned," Slade said. "Yes, I'm glad you told me, and I'll think it over."

"Which means some *ladrones* will need to think hard, and fast," Estaban commented dryly. "But enough of this serious talk. Tonight we seek pleasure only."

Marie jumped up from the table. "Come on, Walt," she said. "Let's take a walk while they're getting ready and dressing. Rosa always has to primp for an hour before going out."

"If I was a dancer and accustomed to running around half naked with nobody thinking anything of it, I'd take no more time than you do," Rosa retorted. "I have to put some clothes on before appearing in public."

Marie giggled and gave her sister an affectionate hug. "Walt doesn't seem to mind," she observed cryptically. "Be seeing you later."

Arm in arm, she and Slade strolled about the quaint Mexican town, similar in some ways but so different in others from its Texas counterpart across the river. Everywhere they were met with smiles and nods and friendly greetings. And glances of admiration were directed toward the sweet-faced girl and her tall, sternly handsome companion. Slade was also the recipient of respectful salutations, which increased in frequency as they sauntered among the curio shops and sidewalk stands.

"There are those who recognize *El Halcon* and do him homage, and the word spreads swiftly," Marie whispered.

"However, it may not be so good for so many to know you," she reflected soberly. "El Halcon has enemies."

"Don't worry your pretty head about it," Slade replied. "Just so long as the right kind of people are not my enemies, I don't pay much mind to the other sort."

"But it worries me to think of your being in constant danger," she said.

"Everybody is," he reminded her. "Sitting in a comfortable, well-drained house with a policeman patroling beneath the window, you still never know what the next moment will bring. And if your number isn't up, nobody can put it up, as I've said before."

"A comforting philosophy, even though it is rather on the fatalistic side," she observed.

"But," he said, "our own actions can put our number up, or often prevent it from being put up. And that is not exactly fatalistic."

"I agree with you," she said, "and it is also comforting."

They walked on, laughing together at the many amusing sights that greeted their eyes.

Slade did not realize it, but that casual stroll was due to have a decided influence on future events.

Gradually they worked around to the river, skirted its curve and walked north at its edge. Finally Marie paused, pointing to where the otherwise placid water swirled and eddied.

"That's the Indian Crossing, a ledge of limestone lying just below the surface of the water," she said. "In real dry seasons it sometimes becomes exposed. Reaches the other side slightly north of the river end of Bruni Stret. The Indians knew it for centuries before the white men found it. They used it to cross stolen cattle over to Mexico. Rustlers still use it, I've heard. Even when the river is high, you can ride a horse across. Wouldn't do to slip, though. The whirlpools would beat you to pieces. Now, with the river low, it's possible to wade clear across, as I have done, I'll show you." She flopped down on the ground, kicked her little dancing slippers free, stripped off her stockings, and, holding her skirts high, stepped boldly into the river.

Slade experienced anxiety as the water foamed and bubbled about her slender ankles; the malestrom of eddies and rapids, especially on the lower side of the ledge, didn't look at all good. But, lithe and graceful, she sped on. Before he knew it she was a hundred yards distant from the shore. In the soft glow of the sunset she seemed a fairy vision walking on the water, and when she turned to wave to him, his breath caught in his throat at her elfin beauty.

"Come back," he shouted. "You're worrying me."

"All right, dear, I wouldn't want to worry you," she called reply, her voice ringing like silver bells over the water. Obediently she turned and swiftly made her way back to where he awaited her. He dried her small but sturdy dancer's feet with a handkerchief and stood gazing thoughtfully at the river while she resumed shoes and stockings. He had heard of the Indian Crossing but had not before realized what a convenient path it provided across the Rio Grande. Might be good sometime to know about the darned thing.

Through the blue and gold of the twilight they walked slowly back to the house, where they found Rosa and Estaban nearly ready to go out.

"Marie, you can ride, of course?" Slade asked suddenly.

"Of course," she replied. "I rode before I could walk. Why?"

"Because tomorrow I'd like for you to ride across to the valley with me and point out what was your father's holding," he explained.

"I'd love to," she agreed. "We'll start early and I'll pack a lunch for us."

"That'll be fine," he said. "Well, here comes Rosa, and the way she loks justifies the time it took. You're beautiful, Rosa!"

"Oh, I'm just a faded old married woman," she replied gaily. "I can't hope to compete with my beautiful little sister. She inherited the famed beauty of the Telos. Our father was a strikingly handsome man and she's a feminine counterpart of him."

"You don't do so bad," Estaban observed cheerfully. "I like 'em a bit on the tall side. Marie's a midget."

"I'm big enough!" Marie countered, glancing at Slade and blushing.

"Well, you do make a fine-looking pair," Estaban conceded. "Everybody says so. All ready? Let's get moving. Any place in particular where you'd like to go?"

"You pick 'em," said Slade. "We'll ride on your trail."

Following Estaban's lead, he threw himself whole-heartedly into the evening's pleasure, banishing, for the time being, care and the vexing problems that confronted him, and thoroughly enjoying himself. He danced with Marie and Rosa and some of the dance floor senoritas, joked with the bartenders and waiters, allowed an orchestra to persuade him to sing a couple of songs, which were received with acclaim. It was late when they finally dropped in at the place Slade had first visited in Marie's company.

"There's El Cascabel at the bar," Estaban said as they sat at a table. "He looks moody."

Slade agreed that the bandit leader did look moody, and impatient about something. He kept casting glances toward the door and appeared to be irritated.

Power finds strange places in which to house itself. Were it not for his unusual eyes, Ralpho Flores might well have been taken for a store clerk or a harmless accountant. No, that wasn't altogether right. There was more to the man than just his eyes. At the moment his small, upright figure dominated the men around him. He stood out because of that inner something that is hard to analyze, hard even to name, but which differentiates one man from another.

Marie, Rosa and Estaban were well-known in that cantina. Almost immediately a gay young vaquero aproached. He bowed low to the girls and his laughing eyes met Slade's.

"Senor, may I have the dance, if it pleases the lady?" he asked.

"Go to it," Slade told him cheerfully. "She's just about worn me out; trying to keep up with her on a dance floor is some chore."

Another of the same calibre instantly claimed Rosa. Estaban picked a senorita from the dance floor. Slade was glad to relax and look over the crowd.

Ralpho Flores turned from the bar and approached the table. "Senor, do you mind if I sit with you?" he asked courteously.

"Be pleased to have you," Slade said, and meant it. He welcomed a chance to study the man more closely.

Flores sat down and ordered wine. Over the rim of his glass he regarded Slade smilingly.

"It is good to take one's ease at times," he said. Slade nodded agreement.

Flores gazed over the gay and laughing crowd. And for the first time, Slade noted a change in his eyes. The hot glow had dimmed, and they were brooding, dream-filled. Flores spoke.

"My people," he said softly. "The day will come when they will be great, and their land a great land. I doubtless will not see it. Perhaps not even you will, young though you are, but it will come."

"I agree with you, sir," Slade replied. "And may it be sooner than we expect."

Flores glanced at him curiously. "You appear friendly to people of my blood," he observed.

The level gray eyes met Flores' gaze squarely. "I am friendly to all people who are good," he replied. Flores shook his head slightly.

"You are a strange man," he said. "One wonders at times if you are really what you are supposed to be." His ingenuous smile flashed out.

"But then who is what he is supposed to be?" he remarked. "Take off the layers of paint we call culture and you find the primal man in all his primal savagery. Perhaps some day we will know each other better and, perhaps—understand each other."

Slade smiled also, but otherwise did not reply.

Abruptly Flores' eyes changed again, and again they seemed to burn. Slade followed his glance, which was fixed on the door.

A man had just entered. He was a big man, tall, broad-shouldered, with lank black hair that reached almost to the collar of his coat. His heavy beard was also lank and black. His eyes in the shadow of his low-drawn hatbrim apeared very dark.

Slade's brows drew together slightly as he regarded him. There was something vaguely familiar about the fellow's carriage, although he could not recall ever seeing him before.

Flores was speaking. "Senor," he said, "you will pardon me? One has just arrived for whom I have been waiting." With a nod and a smile he rose to his feet and crossed the room with quick, light steps. He and the new arrival conversed earnestly, apparently in low tones. Slade was sure the dark eyes in the shadow of the hatbrim glinted in his direction. However, the stranger instantly returned his regard to Flores. A moment later the oddly assorted pair left the cantina together. Slade gazed after their retreaing backs.

"Now where the devil have I seen that jigger before?" he asked of his unresponsive wine glass. "And why is he wearing the phony get-up? Those whiskers are false, I'll bet a hatful of pesos. They hang too straight to be real; not a bit of bristle to them. A false beard never bristles but hangs precisely with a discouraged look. Oh, well, plenty of gents down here who would dance on nothing at the end of a rope if they were recognized by the wrong folks. One of Flores' bunch, I suppose, and it's not surprising that some of them would be a mite bashful about appearing in public au naturel."

Estaban and the girls returned, flushed and gay, Marie sat down beside Slade and held his hand.

"We'd better be going, Walt, if we're to get an early start on our ride," she said. "Don't you think so?"

"I'm ready any time you are," Slade replied. "You and Rosa coming along, Estaban?"

"No need for you to leave if you'd like to stay out a little longer," Marie added.

Estaban shook his head. "I've got to be up early, too," he said. "We'd better be ambling."

Slade was ready to go. Abruptly the night of entertainment and relaxation had fallen flat. He had successfully banished the cares, anxieties and problems which beset him, but now they were back again.

For which he irritably blamed the stranger with the beard. Where had he seen that jigger before! And just what was his status in the web of intrigue. All right to dismiss him as just one of El Cascabel's followers, perhaps bringing a message to Flores, only he wouldn't dismiss that comfortably. There was something about him that belied a minor role. Slade definitely felt that his personality was on a par with that of Flores himself. There had been nothing subsurvient in his attitude toward the bandit leader. Rather, an assuredness that denoted the equal. Flores, Slade believed, was not a man to take second place in an enterprise. But he also believed that Flores was capable of recognizing sound advice and able assistance as things not to be arrogantly shoved aside. Which made him the more dangerous. Ralpho Flores would recognize a superior intelligence but would probably be able to utilize that intelligence to his own advantage. And their brief conversation had convinced Slade that there was more to his self-styled role of liberator than was recognized by a casual observer, such as Estaban, for instance. Flores was first and foremost a bandit leader, with the personal interest of Ralpho Flores his primal objective. But Slade believed he really did take the interest of the Mexican people to heart and would seek to further those interests.

However, he felt that Flores, able though he was, lacked the supple cunning necessary to a successful politician. His methods would be direct, and in such a game directness can easily defeat its own purpose. But he also had an uneasy premonition, based on litle more than instinct—he would call it a hunch—that the bearded stranger did possess those attributes and would prove to be a formidable opponent if he happened to essay that role.

And—also a hunch—Slade was of the opinion that sooner or later the activities of Ralpho Flores would merge with those of the nefarious Land Committee presumably headed by Cale Brandon. He made up his mind to find out, if possible, the personnel of the Land Committee. For he still believed that quite likely Brandon was the front for an abler and more adroit man who was the real moving force behind the Committee and its manipulations. The big question—who the devil was that man? if he really existed. As to that, he so far hadn't the slightest notion. Well, anyhow, the night had passed without untoward incident, and after the recent hectic happenings, that was a relief.

13

THE FOLLOWING MORNING, Estaban brought around a horse for Marie, a sturdy little bay that looked to have speed and endurance. But when Slade appeared mounted on Shadow, there was a chorus of admiration.

"The finest cayuse I ever laid eyes on," Estaban declared.

"What a beauty!" thrilled Marie. "May I pat him?"

"Go ahead," Slade said, "it's okay, Shadow, these folks are all right."

Shadow submitted to their caresses in dignified silence. In fact, he appeared a little bored by such adulation, perhaps because he was so used to it that it had become monotonous.

Slade and Marie left Laredo, after crossing the bridge, by way of Santa Rita Avenue and rode west by north at a leisurely pace, enjoying the warmth of the golden Autumn sunshine. Marie wore Levi's, a soft blue shirt open at the throat, tiny riding boots, and a "J.B." perched jauntily on her dark curls. The garb, Slade thought, did nothing to distract from her attractiveness. Rather, the close fitting shirt and denims enhanced it; Marie Telo certainly did not have to resort to camouflage.

They had little to say to each other, charmed to silence by the mystic beauty of the rangeland. The river was a mile or so to their left, with the brush-grown slopes mistily apparent in the distance to their right. They had covered some miles before Marie announced that they were crossing over what had been her father's holding. They rode on, more slowly, for Slade was studying the terrain. After a while he called a halt and dismounted.

"Want to get a closer look at the ground," he explained. With his knife he cut a square of sod and dug deeply after removing it, running the crumbly earth through his fingers.

"Excellent soil," he announced. "I never saw better. Under right conditions it should grow plenty."

"Too dry," Marie replied. "That's the trouble with all the land hereabouts; not enough rainfall."

"Yes, not enough water," Slade agreed thoughtfully, his gaze fixed on the distant river.

"Come on down," he said. "Let's stretch out and rest a bit while I do some thinking."

For some time, Slade lay smoking a cigarette in silence. Finally he sat up, rolled another cigarette and sat gazing toward the river until the brain tablet was consumed.

"Come on," he said abruptly, "let's ride over there."

He picked her up and tossed her lightly into the saddle.

"You haven't the least notion in the world how strong you are," she exclaimed breathlessly.

"As I told you before, you're easy to handle," he countered.

"Some might say too easy," she retorted cryptically, and sent the bay cantering toward the Rio Grande.

"It's a strange river," Slade observed, gazing at the hurrying water. "Right now, all of a sudden it's rising fast. Not a drop of rain here, but there must be plenty up around the headwaters of the Pecos and Devil River. That's where Rio Grande floodwater comes from."

"But it never overflows the high banks," Marie said.

"No," Slade agreed. "Otherwise this land would be much more productive, like down around Brownsville where the delta is a veritable garden spot. But it did overflow once upon a time. There is a heavy deposit of silt under the grass, the very best soil for growing things. Yes, that's all this land needs—water from the Rio Grande. How far does what was your father's holding extend?"

"For several miles yet," she replied. "There are thousands of acres of it."

"I see," Slade said, his eyes fixed on the distance. There was a satisfied expression on his bronzed face. He was pretty sure that at least one problem was definitely resolved. The pressing problem was what to do about it.

"Suppose we ride up into the hills and have our lunch there," he suggested. "We should be able to find a spring somewhere, and grass for the cayuses. It'll be cool and comfortable up there. The sun's getting hot here."

"That'll be fine," Marie agreed. "I love the hills, and I know them well. I can show you where there's a spring with a little stream running from it in a grass-grown clearing. Less than a mile to the west is a trail that leads to it. From up the slope you can see our *hacienda*, or what used to be ours."

They crossed the valley at a good pace and soon were breasting the slopes, following a crooked trail which slithered in and out between clumps of brush that grew increasingly frequent as they mounted higher. On a little plateau Marie pulled the bay to a halt.

"There it is, over to the west," she said, pointing to a small white ranchhouse that could be seen through a grove of scattered oaks. "There's where I was born. The only home I knew until I went to live with Rosa and Estaban."

Her rich voice quivered a little as she spoke and her expressive eyes were moist.

"You'll be living there again, don't worry,' Slade comforted her. "The land was taken from your father by fraud, and you're going to get it back, that I promise you. And the same goes for some other folks in the section, or I'm making a mighty bad guess," he added.

She smiled wistfully, but her eyes were radiant. "If *El Halcon* says it is so, it *is* so," she said.

"Perhaps, though, you shouldn't be consorting with the notorious outlaw," Slade said playfully, wishing to turn her thoughts into more cheerful channels.

Miss Telo's reaction could be described by no more dignified an appellation than a sniff, daintily feminine, it is true, but nevertheless, a derisive sniff.

"You're about as much an outlaw as Estaban or Padre Juan of the mission across the river," she replied. "Why do you allow people to say such things about you? They aren't true, and you know they aren't."

" 'Sticks and stones may break my bones, but words can never harm me,' " he quoted cheerfully in answer.

"Perhaps not," she conceded, "but it makes me downright angry to think of them being said."

She said it with a dangerous flash of her dark eyes and a clenching of one little fist. Slade had a sudden hunch that Miss Marie Telo could be plenty salty if necessary. The truth of which he was soon to have an impressive example.

From the elevation of the plateau they had an excellent view of the valley for miles and miles. The adobes and small casas looked like doll houses, the cultivated fields were clearly outlined and definite. The great river was a flashing silver band with Laredo nestled in its elbow crook. A mile or so to the east, Slade saw four horsemen riding at a fair pace along the foot of the slopes. Doubtless, they were cowhands from one of the small spreads searching for strays.

"Over west of our holding was the big Bar C ranch," Marie remarked. "It extended for miles and miles along the valley. Then came the Cross-in-a-Box that extended for more miles. But they sold out a little over a year ago. They moved their cattle up north somewhere, I believe."

"Just sold the land, not the cattle?' Slade asked.

"That's right," she replied. "Since then the land has not been tenanted. Just lies there idle, many thousands of acres of it."

"Any idea who they sold to?" Marie shook her head.

"I'm not sure," she said, "but I understand to somebody over east. Whether east Texas or beyond, I don't know. There was a big ranch over to the east beyond the hilly section which is Pablo Navarez' Lazy R that was also sold recently and the cattle moved from it."

"The land beyond the Lazy R is also flat and about the same as this, I believe," Slade remarked.

"That's so," she replied. "Very much the same as here."

Slade nodded thoughtfully, and for some moments was silent. Then, "Guess we might as well get going," he said. "How far to the spring you mentioned?"

"Oh, it's quite a way," she replied. "Well back in the hills. Quiet and peaceful, and nice and lonesome."

"Let's go!" Slade chuckled.

They topped the crest of the slope and for half a mile or more the trail ran across comparatively level ground. Then it dipped into hollows, writhed up other sags and dipped again. Sometimes it was straight for a considerable distance. At others, it turned and slithered like a snake in a cactus patch.

A hollow, then another crest, and they were riding down one of the gently sloping, long, straight stretches that ran for several miles without a bend, with straggles of growth on either side, when Slade's keen ears caught a sound behind them, a sound like to the tripping of fairy feet over the grassheads, and which steadily increased in volume. He quickly catalogued it as the steady beat of fast hoofs the other side of the crest.

Instantly *El Halcon* was very much on the alert. In this lonely terrain, strange horsemen were looked upon somewhat askance until they had proved themselves. Right now, conditions being what they were in the section, it behooved a couple of lone riders to be watchful. He listened intently, recalling the four riders they had seen from the little plateau farther back. He believed the slowly nearing hoofbeats were made by four horses. He turned to his companion.

"Let's speed it up a bit," he suggested casually.

Marie's mind was quick. She cast him a curious glance, nodded and spoke to the bay. Their gait accelerated. But the beat of hoofs to the rear did not fall back. He began to be pretty sure that the unseen riders were pacing them.

Slade kept glancing back toward the crest. Suddenly, four horsemen seemed to float up against the golden pallor of the sky like manikins manipulated against a lighted screen by strings. For an instant they stood out in bold silhouette, every detail delicately outlined, even to the rifles they held at the ready. Then they swept down the slope at a gallop.

Turning back to the front, Slade spoke to Shadow. The great black lengthened his stride; the bay kept pace.

"What is it, Walt?" Marie asked.

"I don't know for sure," he replied, "but somehow it doesn't look good to me. Those gents back there appear mighty anxious to catch up with us. No, it doesn't look good."

It wasn't. A moment later something whined high overhead, followed instantly by the whip-like crack of the distant rifle.

"Thought so," Slade muttered. "Ride, honey, ride!"

Even with the girl on his hands, which complicated matters, Slade was not as yet particularly perturbed. He was confident Shadow could easily outstrip the pursuit, and the bay appeared to have plenty of speed and endurance. Might be a long race, but he believed they'd come out top dog at the finish.

And then it happened, the unpredictable. Slugs were whining past, now, none of them close. It was long shooting from the back of a moving horse and the odds against a hit were long.

Not long enough! Suddenly a scream rent the air, the horrible, high-pitched scream of a stricken horse. The bay reared high.

By a miracle of agility, Slade whirled about and whisked Marie from the saddle even as the bay fell to lie kicking furiously in its death agonies. Slade swore pungently under his breath.

"A blasted one chance in a hundred!" he exclaimed aloud. "This is getting serious."

He was right. The girl's slight weight meant nothing to Shadow, but the awkward distribution of that weight, small though it was, tended to throw him off balance, to render his normally smooth stride choppy. Which inevitably cut down his speed.

There was nothing to do about it. Slade dared not place her behind him, where the weight would be equalized, even if such a maneuver were possible while riding at top speed. There she would be directly exposed to the flying lead, which plays no favorites. He could only hold her in his arms and make the best of it. Maybe before the killers overtook them, they'd reach some spot where he might make a stand. He cursed the trail which, with brush-country contrariness, stretched on and on, straight as an arrow.

A bend loomed in the distance, flanked by a bristle of tall and thick chaparral. Slade watched it draw near with agonizing slowness. Marie spoke for the first time, her voice calm.

"Think we'll make it, Walt?"

"I hope so," he replied. "I've a notion to slow down a bit and drop you off. You can dive into the brush. Anyhow, I don't think they'd hurt you once they saw you are a woman."

"You try it!" she shrilled, tightening her arms around his neck. "Just try it! We're going through this together, to the finish. I wish I'd brought my rifle along; I can shoot."

"Okay," Slade chuckled. "One for all, all for one, as the Three Guardsmen used to say. But those darn slugs are coming close."

They were. One plucked at his sleeve like an urgent

hand. Shadow squealed with anger as another flicked a patch of skin from his glossy haunch. Now the bend was close, but the yelling pursuers were steadily closing the distance. Slade listened to their exultant whoops with satisfaction. They were wildly excited by the chase, and excitement and good judgment don't go together.

"Just you wait!" he muttered between his clenched teeth. "Just let me make it to that bend before you down me! I'll give you something to yell about!"

He made it! With the bullets buzzing around him like angry hornets. Jerking Shadow to a slithering halt, he flipped Marie to the ground, swung from the saddle, slid his Winchester from the boot and raced back to the bend. The pursuers were less than three hundred yards distant when he whipped around it, dropped to one knee and flung the Winchester to his shoulder.

The killers whooped exultantly at sight of him; but the whoops were drowned by a shriek of agony as the rifle spurted flame and a slug tore through the breast of the foremost rider. Even as he toppled from the saddle, the rifle spoke again and a second man fell, shot squarely between the eyes. Then the world exploded in flame and roaring sound and Walt Slade pitched forward on his face, the Winchester dropping from his nerveless hands.

14

THE KILLERS HOWLED with triumph and spurred forward. But instantly there was a small figure beside the fallen ranger. Marie snatched up the rifle, clamped it to her shoulder. The heavy gun bucked, the muzzle flinging up. One of the riders rose in his stirrups, reeled back as if struck by a mighty fist and slumped to the ground. The lone remaining killer yelped as a second bullet slashed along his ribs. He whirled his skating horse and fled back madly the way he had come. Marie sent a final slug whining after him, dropped the rifle and turned to Slade, who was struggling to a sitting position.

"Oh! You're bleeding!" she cried. "Oh, my darling, you're hurt!"

"Not nearly as bad as I would have been if it weren't for you," he mumbled. "I'm okay. Slug grazed my head and knocked me silly. Was plumb paralyzed for a minute.

"What's the matter?" he asked anxiously as she shivered, her teeth clicking together. "You hurt?"

"N—no," she quavered. "It's just that I—I never—shot anybody before."

"Well, you made a darned good beginning," Slade told her as he swabbed at the blood trickling down his temple.

She began dabbing at his bleeding forehead with a small, lacy handkerchief, murmuring over the wound.

"It'll stop in a minute," he reassured her, "my blood clots quickly. I want to see what we bagged. You stay here if you'd rather not look at them."

The big dark eyes flashed. "I don't mind in the least," she replied. "They meant to murder you and got just what was coming to them."

"Good girl!" he applauded. "Yes, you're a girl to ride the river with."

She smiled and dimpled at the highest compliment the rangeland can pay. Together they walked to where the three bodies lay sprawled on the ground.

Two were nondescript looking Border types with nothing outstanding about them. The third, however, was different. His hawk-nosed, lean face was intelligent, his glazing eyes full and protruding slightly from the lids, his mouth tight with a cruel twist to the corners, but otherwise well shaped. Across the back of one muscular hand was a healing wound, the kind of a ragged furrow only a creasing bullet can make.

Slade stared at the wound, his lips pursing in a soundless whistle. There was no doubt in his mind but that he was looking at the hand which had thrust a gun through The Montezuma window in an attempt to murder Wilton Danver! But in the name of Pete, why?

Shaking his head, he began turning out the contents of the dead men's pockets.

"What are you looking for, Walt?" Marie asked curiously.

"Anything that might tie these hellions up with somebody," he answered. "Nothing yet, though. Just some odds-and-ends and a lot of money. They must have been doing well with their murdering."

And then he struck paydirt. From the intelligent-looking man's pocket he drew a folded sheet of stiff paper. Spreading it open he revealed a crisscrossing of lines and a multitude of tiny-lettered notations.

"Looks like some sort of a puzzle," Marie hazarded.

Slade knew it wasn't. It was an accurate, drawn-to-scale copy of the plat shown him by the railroad surveyor. Again he whistled back of his teeth.

So it was a member of the Land Commitee or one of their henchmen who had tried to kill Wilton Danver that night! Slade stared at the paper in bewilderment. The thing just didn't seem to make sense and sent his mind racing in search of a possible explanation. Here was a hitherto unexplored angle. In fact, one that had never occurred to him. He had been told by Sheriff Medford that Danver handled cases for the Land Committee, and Danver had seemed on quite friendly terms with Cale Brandon. A puzzler for fair. He refolded the paper and slipped it in his pocket.

"Keep it for a souvenir," he explained.

They discovered nothing else of significance, but Slade felt he had already learned enough to set him running around in circles.

"Where's that spring of yours?" he asked.

"We passed it a couple of miles back," she replied.

"Okay," he said, straightening up, "let's head for it. All this excitement has made me hungry."

"Me too," she said. "Do you think there's any danger of that man who got away, coming back, perhaps with others?" she asked apprehensively.

"Not him," Slade chuckled. "He won't stop this side of Laredo. If you listen real close you can still hear him whiz! I'll tell Sheriff Medford what happened and he can send a wagon to pick up the carcasses, if he's of a mind to; or leave them to poison the buzzards. Let's go!"

They paused beside Marie's dead horse and Slade removed the rig.

"Shadow will pack it behind the cantle if you don't mind perching in front in my arms."

"That will be perfect," she smiled. "Poor little horse! He was one of Estaban's string. No need to worry about his loss, though; Estaban has plenty more. He has his choice of the hundreds on Don Manuel's ranch."

A narrow rift in the chaparral led to the little clearing where a spring bubbled from under a rock and there was good grass for the horse. Slade produced coffee and a little flat bucket from his saddle pouches and soon had a small fire going and the coffee bubbling.

"We'll have to take turns drinking from the bucket," he said.

" 'And leave a kiss within the cup and I'll not ask for wine,' " she laughingly quoted.

With the elasticity of youth they had thrown off the effects of the recent hectic experience and had a most enjoyable picnic lunch. After which Marie grew silent, her eyes brooding.

"Walt," she said suddenly, "Won't you tell me something about yourself? After—after what we've gone through together, I don't see why we should have any secrets, do you?"

"No, I don't think we should have," he replied soberly, abruptly arriving at a decision. From its secret pocket he slipped the badge of the rangers and handed it to her. She gazed at the famous silver star, the pupils of her eyes dilating.

"So that's what you are," she said slowly. "I'm not surprised. Does anyone else in this section know?"

"Only Sheriff Medford, I hope," Slade answered.

"And I'm beginning to understand why you let the *El Halcon* myth persist," she observed.

"It is helpful to me at times," he replied.

"How did you come to join the rangers?" she asked.

Slade told her. In fact, he told her about everything there was to tell about himself. She listened with rapt attention, her eyes glowing.

"I think I understand, too, why you continue to be a ranger," she said when he paused. "So many opportunities to right wrongs, to obtain justice for those who have been wronged. What you accomplish must give you great satisfaction."

"It does," he admitted. "Right now if I can put a stop to the skullduggery that's going on here in the Rio Grande valley I'll feel mighty good about it."

She nodded. "And perhaps I can help you," she said. "I hear many things in the cantina."

"I wouldn't be surprised if you can," he agreed. "Try and find out all you can about *El Cascabel's* activities. I've a feeling he has something in mind, something that will make for trouble. And I can't help but feel, also, that in some way he's tied up with what's going on this side of the river. Learn all you can."

"I will," she promised, "and Estaban will help me. He has no patience with such as Ralpho Flores."

After a while Slade glanced at the westering sun. "Guess we'd better get going," he said. "I'm afraid you'll be late for work as it is."

"Oh, it doesn't matter if I'm a little late, nobody will say anything," she answered. "Besides, it'll be quiet tonight. Tomorrow night will be different, for tomorrow is payday for the ranches across the river and for many who find employment on this side."

The stars were shining when they reached Laredo. They rode to the stable where Slade kept his horse by way of a quiet side street so as not to attract too much attention. After Shadow was properly cared for they walked to the cantina on Grant Street. Marie skipped off to the dressing room to change while Slade smoked at a table. Soon she reappeared in her dancing costume and they ate together.

The owner, fat and jolly and fiercely-mustached, waddled over to join them. He twinkled snapping little black eyes at Slade.

"Capitan, I am told that wherever you appear there is excitement," he chuckled. "I believe it is so. But I like excitement. What are a couple of spoiled lamps and some broken chairs to such entertainment with a satisfactory ending? I hope you will visit us often."

"And I hope my future visits won't prove as exciting as the last one," Slade smiled. "That one was just a bit too exciting to suit me."

"Excitement, and love, are of life the spice," the owner declared with an airy wave of a plump hand. "Who would wish to be without them!" Still chuckling, he lumbered back to the bar.

"'Pears to be a right hombre," Slade commented.

"He is," said Marie. "Everybody likes Miguel. He's a Texas-Mexican, old stock. He's very good to me. Always has somebody walk me across the bridge when I finish work. He feels very bad about what's going on in the valley."

"He has a right to," Slade replied. 'But I've a notion that before the business is finished, some other gents are going to feel worse," he added grimly. "Well, I'll be seeing you, honey. I want to look up Sheriff Medford."

"Be careful of yourself, dear."

"I will."

Sheriff Medford was in his office when Slade arrived there. He listened to what the ranger had to tell him and swore sulphurously.

"And you figure you got the hellion who tried to kill Wilton Danver?"

"I think that was the one Marie got," Slade replied.

"That little gal's a wonder!" the sheriff exclaimed admiringly.

"You can say that a couple of times," Slade returned. "She sure saved my bacon for me; I was knocked cold for a few seconds. Are you going to pack the bodies in?"

"Reckon I'd better, so as they can hold an inquest," the sheriff decided morosely. "Just a waste of time, except that I want a look at them myself, especially the one who tried to do for Danver. May recognize the sidewinder."

"And perhaps who he was associated with," Slade interpolated.

"Yes, that's an idea," agreed the sheriff. "Wonder why in blazes he tried to do it?"

"I'd like the answer to that one," Slade replied. "I'm positive that he was associated with the Land Committee. But of course it might have meant a personal grudge of some sort; that angle must be considered. By the way, can you tell me who makes up the Land Committee?"

"Well, there is Brandon, who 'pears to run it," the sheriff answered. "Then there are three jiggers who came here shortly after he did and became associated with him in his real estate business. Never seem to do anything much but are in his office. Keep to themselves mostly and don't mix much with folks. Named Tom Logan, Silas Marsch, and Jim Kraus. Then there's a bar owner over on San Agustine Avenue named Doty, another one on Bruni Street, and a feller who owns a small spread up to the northeast, Harry Brophy. They make up the committee, so far as I know."

"Nobody very prominent or outstanding, I gather," Slade remarked.

"Guess that's about right," agreed the sheriff. "Ordinary sort of jiggers. I don't know anything about the three who came here from the Panhandle, or so they say, but the others have never been conspicuous in any way and have never been known to do anything off-color."

"Sometimes honest and decent individuals, but not too bright, are induced to join some venture without realizing its true nature," Slade observed thoughtfully. "Brandon and his associates may have sucked them in to lend an aura of respectability to the enterprise and to intimate that it is approved by local opinion."

"You may have something there," admitted the sheriff.

"Doubtless Brandon and the three from the Panhandle are the prime movers in the business, and the brains," Slade continued. "And I'd say they have a lot of hired riff-raff to do their dirty work. Brandon showed he's not as smart as he could be by taking part in the assault on Felipe Cardena. Has a sadistic streak in his makeup, I'd say. He was using the whip and he seemed to enjoy it. But, blast it! I still can't see him having the brains to engineer such a project. I wonder if there is somebody back of him?"

"Who?" asked the sheriff.

"If I had the answer to that, I'd have the answer to a number of things," Slade said.

"You'll get it," the sheriff predicted.

"Glad you have so much confidence in me, even though it may not be justified," Slade smiled.

"As the Mexican peons would say, confidence in *El Halcon* is never unjustified," said the sheriff.

"They're prejudiced in my favor because I've been able to help a few of them," Slade rejoined.

"Jim McNelty himself is sort of prejudiced, then," said the sheriff. "And that old coot would look with suspicion on an angel fresh from Heaven and insist that he prove himself."

Slade laughed. "I sure wish I knew who that jigger is who met Ralpho Flores in Nuevo Laredo the other night," he said. "I've got a hunch that he's a somebody and with connections up here. Also that he has influence with Flores who, in my opinion, while cunning and resourceful is not too smart and might be induced to do something his better judgment tells him is not the thing to do. I'm sure I've seen that fellow before, but for the life of me I can't recall when or where. Well, as I've said before, time that grinds the rocks will tell us all."

He stood up, stretching his long arms above his head to almost touch the ceiling with his fingertips.

"I'm going to call it a night," he said. "See you tomorrow, fairly early I expect."

"Okay," replied the sheriff. "I'll send a couple of deputies and a wagon to pack those bodies in. Be seeing you."

15

THE FOLLOWING MORNING Sheriff Medford had a visitor, a youngish man with a lean face, thin, tight lips and hard, watchful eyes.

"Sheriff, I am John Cradlebaugh," he introduced himself. "I am from the Land Office. I am here to investigate the condemnation of land claimed by way of a Spanish grant by one Sebastian Telo, deceased. A local outfit here, known as the Land Committee, has, or had, an option on that land. The option is being cancelled and the Office is conducting a thorough investigation of the matter. Also, at the behest of Captain James McNelty of the Texas Rangers, an appeal of the lower court ruling is being made. I would like to speak with the lower court judge who handed down the decision."

"Okay," replied the sheriff. "I'll take you to Parkinson. He's in his office right now."

Judge Parkinson was tall and angular, with a long, scrawny neck that rose out of a very low collar, and a large head, scantily covered with hair—a head that gave a physical as well as a mental effect of hardness. He was a person on whom dignity lay heavily, but as the brittle voice of the investigator bit at him, questioning, questioning, he lost his aplomb. His face twitched, his mouth sagged. By the time the Land Office man got through with him he was sweating profusely and his hands were shaking.

"That will be all, sir, for the present," Cradlebaugh finally said, taking a folded sheet from the small satchel he carried. "Here is a subpoena from the office of the Attorney General directing that all the papers relative to the matter be turned over to me. Send them to the sheriff's office, all of them. I'll pick them up there. I'll see you again."

He rose to his feet, apparently did not see the hand the judge extended, for he turned his back on him and walked from the office.

"Fraud!" he snapped to Sheriff Medford when the

latter joined him outside. "Palpable fraud. Perjured testimony. Very likely, forged documents. Wait till I get at the bottom of this mess! The seat of somebody's pants will ring like a bell. By the way, Sheriff, I have been informed that you are consorting with a man who, in certain quarters, at least, has the reputation of being a notorious outlaw. I desire to speak with that man."

"Okay," said the sheriff. "Chances are, he's at my office right now; I'm expecting him this morning. You can judge him for yourself."

"I will," the investigator promised emphatically.

Slade was in the office when they arrived. Medford introduced Cradlebaugh. The investigator smiled, a very pleasant smile. Abruptly he was a quite different man from the man who brought Judge Parkinson to his knees. He extended his hand.

"Mr. Slade," he said, "it is a pleasure to know you. I believe we have a friend in common in the person of Captain Jim McNelty."

"Anybody who is a friend of Captain Jim's is a friend of mine," Slade said as they shook hands.

"Thank you," said Cradlebaugh. "I read your letter to Captain Jim. Have you any further information for me?"

"Yes," Slade replied. "I have the motive for you."

"The motive?"

"Yes," Slade repeated. "The motive behind the skullduggery that's been going on here. The holding company back of the building railroad, a big Eastern syndicate, plans a vast irrigation project here, which will greatly increase land values."

"Do you think the syndicate in question is involved?" Cradlebaugh asked. Slade shook his head.

"I don't think so," he replied. "The syndicate is not interested in the small holdings here, although in the aggregate, those holdings are far from small. As you doubtless know, the syndicate has acquired options on all state land hereabouts. They have also purchased, at a fair market price, several big ranches. They have many thousands of acres at their command, acres they will sell or lease to the farmers from the East who will soon be pouring in. Of course, they tried to keep the project secret, to prevent land prices from skyrocketing. They have been successful, to an extent, but somewhere there was a leak which reached the wrong people. The Land Committee, so called, stands to reap a huge profit if allowed to get away with what they plan. This section of the valley will become a garden spot."

Slade was right in his prediction. Before many years had passed what was once an area of arid cattle land had been, by extensive irrigation, transformed into a fertile agricultural section which grew and shipped thousands of carloads of vegetables, especially Bermuda onions, each year.

"Well, before I'm finished I expect to get some fraud indictments and convictions," said Cradlebaugh.

"And I hope to get convictions for something much more serious," Slade interpolated.

"What?"

"Murder! I am convinced that Sebastian Telo was murdered to prevent him from appealing the lower court ruling," Slade replied. "And there were others—little people whose killing didn't create much of a stir. And if I don't get a break soon, there will probably be more killings. The situation here has gotten totally out of hand, with developments that the promoters of the scheme very likely didn't anticipate. But they're in too deep to pull out and will stop at nothing to save their own hides."

"You have no proof against anybody?"

"I have no proof of anything against anybody other than assault," Slade answered. "However, I trust that condition will not obtain indefinitely."

"It won't," Sheriff Medford declared emphatically.

"I think you're right," said Cradlebaugh. "I'm convinced the field work here is in competent hands. Captain McNelty thinks so, too. He said it's just a matter of time."

"But time's running out," Slade said. "And now, sir, I would suggest that you don't altogether divulge your conclusions just yet. Act a bit uncertain. Perhaps we'll be able to lure the hellions into a feeling of false security and as a result they may get careless and tip their hand."

"I'll do it," promised Cradlebaugh. "That's a good

suggestion. You hand out the powders and I'll follow your lead. Don't you think that's a good idea, Sheriff?"

"Couldn't be any better," replied the old peace officer. "Let Slade handle things and we'll come out on top."

Late that evening, the three bodies were brought in by the deputies and laid out in the coroner's office for inspection. Crowds of citizens filed through the office for a look. A couple of bartenders were of the opinion that they had served one or more of the individuals, but were vague as to when and where. The same went for a waiter or two.

Sitting in a shadowy corner, Walt Slade studied the expressions of those who passed in review.

"I've a notion there are a few folks who know more than they care to reveal," he confided to Sheriff Medford. "Well, you can't blame them much, the way things have been going hereabouts of late. They probably consider it might be unhealthy to get mixed up in the business."

Among those who visited the office was Wilton Danver. For some minutes he gazed at the body of the man whose hand was marked by a bullet wound. There was a slight pucker between his brows. Finally he shook his head and left without comment. Slade's gaze followed him out the door, a thoughtful and slightly puzzled look in his eyes.

Slade met Marie after she finished work and spent the night at Estaban's house. When he entered the sheriff's office the following afternoon, that peace officer was awaiting him.

"Well, things have really begun to break," he said, waving Slade to a chair.

"Yes? How's that?" Slade asked as he began the manufacture of a cigarette.

"Cale Brandon was found murdered this morning," the sheriff replied.

Slade stopped his cigarette-making in mid-air.

"Murdered!"

"That's right, in a hallway down on Zaragoza Street. Had a knife stuck through his throat."

Slade whistled, and stared at the sheriff.

"What do you think of that?" Medford asked.

"I think," Slade said slowly, "that Brandon pulled a doublecross on somebody, or tried to, and last night he collected his pay."

Sheriff Medford regarded him curiously. "Got any idea who might have done it?" he asked.

"Not an idea I'd care to talk about, at present," Slade replied.

"Then you have got an idea."

"Hardly an idea," Slade said. "Rather, a nebulous hunch with nothing but thin air to stand on."

"When did you get the hunch?"

"The minute you told me Cale Brandon had been murdered."

There was a baffled look on the sheriff's face. "You can say less when you talk than any man I ever met," he growled.

"It's a gift," Slade smiled. "Or perhaps, it's just that I haven't anything to say."

Medford snorted and reached for his pipe.

"By the way," he said, "Felipe Cardena dropped in this morning. Had something interesting to tell me and asked me to tell you."

Slade looked expectant and the sheriff regaled him with an account of Felipe's adventure with the six raiders who invaded his adobe. Slade chuckled with appreciation.

"That old jigger's okay," he said. "I'd liked to have been there to see it. I'll bet those hellions have still got the shakes."

"Three of 'em haven't," the sheriff returned grimly. "Felipe recognized those carcasses in the coroner's office as members of the bunch. He seemed plumb pleased."

Slade chuckled. "I imagine he was. Did you tell him about Brandon?" The sheriff nodded.

"What did he say to that?"

"He rolled his eyes up piously to the sky and said, 'El Dios is just,' and left smiling."

Slade shook with laughter. "I've a notion," he said, "that Felipe Cardena has a sense of humor."

"The inquest will be held in about an hour," said the sheriff. "You are expected to attend. What about the girl?"

"Leave her out of it," Slade answered. "She was around the bend when I started shooting."

"Okay, I'll fix it with Doc Beard. No sense in dragging her into it that I can see. Only she ought to get some credit for saving you from being plugged."

"She doesn't want it, and she wouldn't relish the publicity," Slade replied.

The inquest didn't take long. The jury complimented Slade on doing a good chore. It 'lowed that Cale Brandon met his death at the hands of a party or parties unknown and—a typical cow-country rider—supposed that the sheriff should try to run the hellions down, but who gave a hang, anyway!

"Senor Brandon wasn't over popular," the sheriff commented.

John Cradlebaugh appeared shortly afterward. "Well, it looks like my case may fall to the ground," he said. "The other members of the committee will band together and swear that Brandon was the moving force and that they just obeyed orders and didn't know what was going on. Chances are they'd get away with it before a jury."

"Possibly," Slade conceded, "but I've a notion they won't get away with a murder charge when and if it is filed against them. In that eventuality, somebody is very likely to talk to save his own hide. And I hope to have plenty of corroborative evidence when I file the charge."

"If you manage to stay alive that long," grunted the sheriff. "But maybe things will cool down with Brandon out of the picture."

"They won't," Slade declared. "The real head of the outfit is still running around loose, and he's a heck of a lot more dangerous and resourceful than Brandon who, after all, was just another hired hand, the field man who took care of the dirty work."

Both Medford and Cradlebaugh looked expectant, but Slade did not elaborate.

"I talked with Wilton Danver, the lawyer who handled the Telo land case for the committee," Cradlebaugh continued. "He was very cooperative. He said that Brandon gathered the evidence and brought forward the witnesses who testified and that he had no reason not to believe everything was authentic, which seems reasonable."

"Who were the witnesses?" Slade asked. He had already learned from Marie and Rosa, but he wanted the investigator's corroboration.

"A man named Pablo Navarez, a ranch owner, and his major-domo and another employee," replied Cradlebaugh. "Navarez testified that Telo admitted to him that his forebears never had a grant, that they were nesters from the beginning. The other two corroborated what Navarez said. Navarez produced a letter he claimed was written him by Telo, in which was admission that Telo never had a grant and asked Navarez to ascertain the exact status of his holding from the Land Office. Appears Navarez was negotiating with Telo for the purchase of Telo's holding and it was, of course, necessary for him to learn if Telo had clear title. I understand Telo denied he had written the letter and swore he had never held such a conversation with Navarez. But with three witnesses contradicting him, Judge Parkinson refused to believe his story. I think all three witnesses lied and that the letter was a forgery, which may be hard to prove, but it would appear Danver acted as attorney in good faith. I understand he won a case for Navarez against the Land Committee."

"Did Danver happen to mention why the committee wanted Navarez' holdings?" Slade asked. "His land could not be irrigated from the Rio Grande."

"He was vague about that," Cradlebaugh replied. "He said Brandon mentioned something about artesian wells that would supply water for irrigation."

"If he'd drilled one through to China he might have gotten something," Slade observed dryly. "There would be no subterranean reservoir under pressure there, which is necessary to an artesian well. All drainage would be unobstructed to the bed of the Rio Grande. Even an elementary knowledge of geology would prove that."

"I think I'll have a little talk with Senor Pablo Navarez," he added.

16

As SHERIFF MEDFORD SAID, when things really started moving they moved fast. Several uneventful days passed, then one morning when Slade dropped in at the office he found an elderly cattleman there, whom he recognized as one of the poker players who sat with Brandon and Wilton Danver the night of his first visit to The Montezuma. The sheriff introduced him as Rolf Austin.

"Rolf was just telling me of a good buy he made," said Medford.

"Yep. Best buy I ever made," said Austin. "Pablo Navarez' spread. He rode over to my place and offered it to me, cows and everything, for a price I considered dirt cheap. Said he was tired of the section and wanted to move. It rounds out my holding nicely. Best buy I ever made. I hired his hands to run it, except his majordomo and a couple of the older fellers, who were going with him. I stopped at his casa on my way to town, but he'd already pulled out. Yep, I figure it was quite a bargain."

After Austin left, the sheriff turned to Slade. "And what does that mean?" he asked.

"It means," Slade replied, "that Navarez was tipped off to get in the clear, and fast. I expect he's halfway to the other 'end of Mexico by now. Another lead gone skalleyhooting. I'd figured to try to see Navarez tomorrow. Seems the hellions are always a jump ahead of me."

"Well, anyhow, the Telo gals will get their spread back," the sheriff said. "Cradlebaugh is sure of it."

"Yes, but unless I can prove something against the other members of that blasted committee, a lot of other poor folks who were frightened or maneuvered out of their holdings won't get them back," Slade said morosely. "Cradlebaugh admits he's stumped. He said somebody did some mighty clever legal work and covered up beautifully. That even if he could persuade somebody to bring litigation, he is not at all sure of winning."

"So things don't look so good," commented the sheriff.

"No, but I still have an ace in the hole that I may get a chance to play," Slade said. "An ace known as *El Cascabel.*"

"What the devil!" exploded the sheriff. *"El Cascabel?"*

"Yes," Slade replied. "I believe that the big phony-whiskered gent whom I am convinced is the real head and moving force of the Land Committee had persuaded Ralpho Flores to do something. Something he may now, in the light of recent developments, consider not expedient. But I believe that if he really sold Flores the idea, that Flores will act on his own account. He's not the sort to take orders from anybody, and he's out for Flores, first, last and always. If he believes he can profit from the business, whatever it is, he'll go through with it, no matter what the Land Committee has to say. I've learned that he has not been seen around Nuevo Laredo for several days. Quite likely he's rounding up his *bandidos* and geting them set to act."

"But what the devil could he have in mind?" wondered the sheriff. "A big cattle steal from this side of the river?"

"Possibly, but I rather doubt it," Slade said. "I've a notion it'll be something more spectacular than cow rustling. I hope to learn more soon."

Slade decided to play another hunch. "Where on Zaragosa Street is that hallway in which you found Brandon's body?" he asked.

"The building is on the southwest corner of an alley just east of San Agustin Avenue," the sheriff replied. "It's a sort of roominghouse, almost empty, for water-front characters. I questioned one or two of them but they didn't know anything, or if they did, they wouldn't tell. What you got in mind?"

"I think I'll look it over," Slade said. "Might learn something."

"I doubt it," grunted Medford. "Folks are close-mouthed down there; they never know anything."

"Somebody might let something slip," Slade said. He didn't tell Medford just what he had in mind, for if he did the sheriff would very likely wish to accompany him, and he preferred to go it alone.

He left the office and walked in the golden Autumn sunshine, thinking deeply and trying to weave the recent developments into something of a correlated pattern. Cale Brandon had been an unsavory personality and his getting his comeuppance could be catalogued as an example of retributive justice; Brandon had it coming. But Brandon had also been the key figure in Slade's investigation. His unexpected removal left a vacuum that must somehow be filled.

Slade discarded the other known members of the committee as mere hired hands who obeyed orders and asked no questions, content to let a superior intelligence direct the moves they carried out. His speculation centered on the mysterious "unknown" who wove in and out of the shadows like an evil spirit transplanted from the age of the Medicis. Although he had made no mention of the fact to Sheriff Medford, Slade was convinced that he now knew the identity of that sinister individual. Which was something, at least. He knew on whom to concentrate, but unless he was able to obtain something resembling definite proof, that slippery customer might well wriggle out of the noose. Well, the next move he had in mind might possibly get some results. Another hunch, but sometimes hunches proved to be straight ones.

The truth of the matter was that Walt Slade's "hunches" were built on the exploration of all angles and the careful analysis of conditions, events and developments. For instance, Cale Brandon was murdered in a certain locality, which made that locality of interest. Why had Brandon been there, a section which would certainly be considered off-beat for a prominent and successful, though controversial, businessman. That portion of Zaragoza Street and the waterfront were the stamping grounds of characters that were not the sort one would consider logical associates of a man in his position. Certainly not the sort he would deliberately seek out. But Brandon had been where they habitually congregated, and there he had met his death. The inference was, Slade believed, that he had gone there to meet someone. One of the waterfront hangers-on? Slade did not think so. Could it have been to attend a meeting rather than to meet somebody? Slade was intrigued by that possibility, and from that had developed his hunch. He was resolved to follow the hunch, later.

Eventually his stroll led him to the International Bridge. At the middle of the span he leaned on the railing and gazed down at the hurrying water and listened to the sob and moan of the swollen river.

Laredo had a police department of sorts composed, in equal numbers, of Mexicans and Americans. As Slade leaned against the rail, the police chief himself came sauntering along. He was a pleasant-faced, affable man of middle age. He greeted Slade with a genial wave of his hand.

"Howdy, cowboy?" he said. "Having a look at old debbil river? Looks like she might be getting ready for another rampage, and every time she does, I get worried about this darn bridge. She'll go out some time, sure as blazes. When the river is real swole up I've seen only the tops of the lamp-posts visible. Let a real sockdollager come roaring down and she *will* go out. I'll bet a hatful of pesos on it."

"The situation could easily be remedied at no great cost," Slade observed.

"How's that?" asked the chief, looking interested.

"It would be quite simple," Slade replied. "Replace these riveted steel railings and side sections with bolted aluminum sheets and railings. When a bad flood threatens, they could be easily removed and the side sections carried to safety, aluminum being very light and removing the bolts no difficult chore. Stripped in that manner, the bridge would present virtually no obstruction to the current and its floating debris."

The chief looked even more interested. Suddenly his eyes twinkled.

"Name's Slade, isn't it, sometimes known as *El Halcon?*" he questioned.

"The name is right, and I have been called *El Halcon,*" Slade smilingly replied.

The chief extended his hand. "I don't know about the *El Halcon* sheep dip," he said. "Sheriff Medford don't seem to put much stock in it, and as a matter of fact, neither do I. But I think you've got a head on your shoulders and what you've just told me is darned interesting. Tell you what, there is a council meeting tonight at nine o'clock. Could you see your way to attend and express your views to the council? There are some educated fellers on it and they'll understand what you have to say better than I do. What say?"

"I'll be pleased to attend," Slade accepted the invitation.

"Fine!" said the chief. He shook hands again. "I'll be seeing you, then." With a nod and a smile he sauntered on. Slade remained gazing down at the hurrying water.

"Looks like something in the nature of a side issue," he told the turgid river, "but you can't tell. Official backing of any kind is never to be discounted." He resumed his stroll, heading for Nuevo Laredo and Estaban's domicile.

"I haven't seen you for three whole days," Marie greeted him reproachfully.

"Been sort of busy," Slade returned lightly. "I'm here now."

"Yes, and I'll expect you to walk me home tonight," she said, blushing a little and slanting him a glance through her lashes.

"I'll be right on the job," he promised. "And I'll walk you to work this evening."

Slade attended the council meeting. Realizing that there were men present who would understand what he was talking about, he used technical language dealing with points of moment, stresses and strains, resistances, hydraulic volumes, mounting thrusts, etc. The council appeared much impressed and after he had finished, shook hands all around.

When he took his departure, the police chief remarked, "There are some terrapin-brained gents who say that young feller is a notorious outlaw. Well, all I can say is I hope we get a few more outlaws of the same sort. We can use 'em."

"Outlaw, the devil!" snorted one elderly member who had listened with absorbed interest. "He's a right hombre, or I never saw one. I'm for him till the last brand is run."

As a matter of fact, Slade's plan was adopted to the letter. Today, when flood threatens, only thirty minutes are required to remove the aluminum railings and side sections and carry them to safety. Even the monumental plaque in honor of "The Womanhood of All the Americas," placed in the middle of the bridge by the Pan American Round Table, is made of aluminum and is removable.

17

Shortly after midnight found Slade walking Zaragoza Street. Without difficulty he located the hallway he sought and took up a position in the thick darkness of the north mouth of the alley which crossed the street, from where he could see the entrance to the hallway. The alley mouth across the street to the east of the hallway was a black square into which seeped the palest glimmer of starlight.

A tedious hour passed and part of another, with nothing happening. The street was deserted, but from the distance came the hum of voices sometimes raised in altercation or ribald song. Slade began to grow heartily tired of the endless waiting with no results.

And then he saw four shadowy figures approaching from the west. They entered the hallway and were instantly swallowed by its gloom. A moment later a faint bar of radiance seeped across the alley to the south, a few yards from its mouth. Evidently somebody had lit a lamp in a room, a window of which faced on the alley. Slade continued to wait, contemplating what his next move should be.

From the west two more figures materialized to also enter the hallway. Undoubtedly a meeting of some sort was being held in that lighted room.

Suddenly he leaned forward, every nerve tense. From the west a lone figure had appeared, a tall and broad-shouldered man with his hatbrim drawn low over his eyes. A vagrant beam from a street light glinted on his black beard. He too entered the hallway. Slade thought he heard the soft click of a closing door. And unless it was his over-active imagination in play, the entrance of the hallway glowed the merest trifle an instant before the door closed.

Now what the devil should he do? He was consumed by intense curiosity as to what was going on in that room. How to find out! He glanced up and down Zaragoza Street. Nobody was in sight. That dim bar of light seeping across the alley drew him like a lode stone. Again he studied his surroundings, made up his mind. With swift, light steps he glided across the street and into the opposite alley mouth. Flattened against the wall of the building, he listened intently. No sound broke the stillness. With the greatest caution he edged along the wall toward where the shaft of light drifted through a crack between shutters that were not tightly closed. And as he drew near the crack, he caught a soft murmur of voices. Another moment and he could peer into the lighted room.

Around a table sat seven men. At the head, sat the big man who had entered last. Now, however, he did not wear a beard. That lay on the table before him. His hair was not black and lank but tawny, inclined to curl and neatly cut. His eyes, which in the uncertain light of the cantina appeared black, now showed darkly blue. Slade was not in the least surprised to recognize Wilton Danver.

One of the men, a hatchet-faced individual in "store clothes," was speaking in a high, nasal voice.

"Ever since that big hellion showed up here we've had trouble," he creaked. "He's got the Mexicans with their bristles up and fighting back. He has old Medford hypnotized, and the same goes for that infernal Land Office snoop. Everybody he gets in touch with, he right away has under his thumb. I heard he attended a council meeting tonight. What went on there I don't know, but I'll bet a hatful of pesos that we'll soon learn and that it will be something unpleasant."

"Yes, he's trouble, Martin, and he must be eliminated," Danver said.

"We've tried eliminatin' him, and what has it got us?" Martin sneered. "We've lost half a dozen men, including Cale Brandon. How he did for Brandon I can't imagine, but I'll bet my bottom dollar he did it."

"You'd lose," replied Danver, his voice harsh, metallic. "Brandon got exactly what was coming to him. What anybody else who tries to double-cross me will get."

The men at the table stared. "What the devil do you mean, Danver?" Martin demanded.

"I mean," Danver said, "that Brandon planned to do away with me and take over. With things rolling along nicely, or so it seemed, he figured he didn't need me any more and had Henderson, that gun-slinging side-kick of his, try to shoot me in the back while I was playing cards in The Montezuma. That's one thing I'll have to hand Slade; he saved my life that night. At first, Brandon had me believing that the whole thing was a plant engineered by Slade to get in my good graces. Yes, I believed him, at first, until I found out different. I braced Brandon the other night, told him he was a grass-crawling rat and handed him what he had coming, that's all. Any more questions?"

There was an uncomfortable silence, the table's occupants glancing from one to another, askance. Danver smiled thinly and relaxed in his chair. The fingers of his left hand, which had been caressing the left lapel of his long black coat, dropped back to the table.

"What about Flores?" asked Martin.

"I think I'll tell Flores to pull in his horns," Danver replied contemplatively. "I rather doubt that what he has in mind would do us any good right now, and it might do us harm."

"I'm not so sure of that," said the argumentative Martin, who appeared to be the spokesman for the others. "Folks change their opinions mighty fast, and if they figure the valley Mexicans are to blame they'll quick get riled up against them, no matter what's happened before."

"I'll think on it," said Danver. "I haven't been able to locate Flores for the past few days. He's dropped out of sight for some reason or other. He does that every now and then, though, when he's off on a raid or something, so I don't think much of it. He'll show up and then I'll have a talk with him. I managed to put a little stiffening in Judge Parkinson's backbone and he's ready to fight back. I wonder where the devil Johnson is, he should have shown up before now. About that blasted Cradlebaugh—"

Slade had become so engrossed in the conversation that he completely forgot that he was outlined against the bar of light streaming through the open window. He whirled at the sound of a stealthy step behind him. Just in time he saw the gleam of the downward slashing knife. He flung up his hand to ward the blow and his arm, hard and rigid as a bar of steel, caught the knifer's descending wrist. The hand flew open and the blade tinkled on the ground. He lunged forward and they closed in a deadly grapple.

Instantly Slade knew he was fighting for his life. The knifer was a big man and muscled like an ox. Slade got a grip on his throat in time to stifle the rising yell. The other went for his gun, but Slade clamped his wrist to his side. They wrestled furiously, back and forth, their boots clattering on the cobbles. Inside the room, there was a banging of overturned chairs.

The knifer tore free and leaped back. Two hands flashed down and up. Two guns boomed, Slade's first by a split second. A bullet fanned his face. The knifer reeled back with a gurgling cough and fell. Slade whirled and raced down the alley. Behind him, a gun cracked. The bullet came close. Another and another, lending wings to his already flying feet. With a gasp of relief he whisked around a corner and sped east at top speed, stumbling over broken stones. He turned the corner into San Bernardo Avenue and fled north, praying that the devils hadn't thought to run east on Zaragoza and cut him off. He passed the intersection without hindrance, reached Grant Street and whipped around the corner, slackening his speed. He had caught his breath by the time he reached the cantina where Marie danced. He pushed through the swinging doors and dropped into a chair at a table, thankful for the chance to rest his aching legs.

Miguel, the owner, bowlegged over to join him. Easing his huge form into a chair he jerked his thumb toward Marie dancing with a young vaquero, and rolled his eyes soulfully.

"Ah! She is lovely!" he chanted. "Beautiful as the first flower of spring swaying in the dawn wind. Capitan, you are the—how you say it—perro afortunado."

"Lucky dog," Slade translated. "Yes, Miguel, I think I am, in more ways than one."

Miguel chuckled and ordered wine for two, on the house. Still chuckling he waddled off. Slade rolled a cigarette and sat thinking and waiting for Marie to finish her dance.

Well, anyhow he had corroborated what he suspected. Wilton Danver was his man. And when he saw the bullet wound across the hand of Henderson, the dead killer, Danver caught on to Gale Brandon's doublecross and gave Brandon his comeuppance. But where the devil was Ralpho Flores? And what sort of an egg was he hatching? Slade didn't have the answer to those questions and fervently wished that he had. He suffered an uneasy premonition that when he got the answers they wouldn't be pleasing. Especially if he happened to get them too late.

He chuckled as he envisioned the bewilderment and consternation in the Zaragoza Street room. He did not believe the knife wielder, quite likely the man, Johnson, mentioned by Danver, who arrived late for the meeting and spotted him, had talked before he died. The slug evidently got him through the throat. If he didn't, Danver and his bunch must be sorely puzzled as to what happened in the alley outside the window. Apprehensive, too, not knowing just what did happen or how much of their talk was overheard and by whom. Well, if they got jumpy enough, somebody might let something slip. Which could possibly simplify matters.

Her dance finished, Marie skipped over and dropped into a chair, rosy and breathless and smiling.

"I was beginning to think you wouldn't show up," she said sipping her wine. "Where have you been?"

"Just running around," he replied lightly, reflecting that he certainly had been running. His legs still ached.

"You're always on the go," she said. "Don't you ever get a chance to rest?"

"If I don't, who's to blame?" he countered.

Marie blushed, and didn't answer.

"How long before you're finished here?" he asked.

She glanced at the clock. "Less than an hour. Would you like to dance?"

"I'd rather sit this one out," he decided.

"So would I," she agreed. "Miguel's getting ready to bring more wine. He's developed a great liking for you."

"Miguel's okay," Slade said. "I believe he has the soul of a poet, although you might not think it to look at him. He likened you to the first flower of spring swaying in the dawn wind. I thought the comparison very apt."

Marie gave a little merry trill of laughter, and intoned words that Slade didn't forget and which, much later, were to seep into a very popular song.

"Hold me like a flower for one little hour!"

18

AN ASTOUNDED MAN was Sheriff Tobe Medford the following afternoon when Slade recounted his adventures of the night before.

"Wilton Danver!" he exclaimed. "I can't believe it. He's the last person I know of I'd have run such a brand on."

"You can never judge by outward appearances or outward manifestations," Slade said. "He had me thoroughly fooled, too, for quite a while. Like you, I hadn't the slightest notion he was mixed up in the business, and I was just as thoroughly astonished to find that he was. I admit I was a mite surprised when Marie and Rosa told me he was the lawyer who handled the Telo case for the Land Committee, but I thought he had probably acted in good faith, as he later maintained he did. A lawyer can make mistakes and be fooled the same-as anybody else. It was only after I learned other things that the significance of his pressing the suit for the Land Committee was apparent."

"How'd you come to get a line on him?" the sheriff asked.

"By way of a series of seemingly inconsequential incidents," Slade explained. "I first got to puzzling over him, although at the time I didn't know he was the man I was puzzling over, when he came into the Nuevo Laredo cantina to meet Ralpho Flores. That phony beard he was wearing got me interested, and I was sure from his mannerisms that I'd seen him somewhere before. I couldn't get him out of my mind. Remember the night he came in to look at Henderson's body?"

"Henderson, the sidewinder Marie plugged up on the trail," interpolated the sheriff. "The one with the bullet wound across the back of his hand?"

"That's right. When Danver spotted that bullet wound, all of a sudden his eyes blazed like fire and his face twisted; for a moment he looked like a maniac. Henderson, judging from what was said last night, was Cale Brandon's close friend and associate. As soon as he saw that slash across the back of his hand, Danver caught on to the doublecross. He knew that Brandon was out to get him and take over. Brandon, cunning in a way, but otherwise rather stupid, figured that he could finish up the business without Danver and thereby profit more, so he tried to get rid of Danver. Honor among thieves! A typical example. Danver, of course, is the prime mover in the business. It was Danver, no doubt of that, who conceived the scheme in the first place. I expect a thorough investigation of his past will reveal that he had some connection with the Eastern syndicate. Perhaps he was their attorney in local affairs in Louisiana. He saw that if he could acquire all the loose parcels of land here in the valley at a low price, he could profit immensely when the irrigation project was put into effect and land values skyrocketed. Just a sly business deal in the beginning."

"Uh-huh, the kind a natural born ladrone goes in for," snorted the sheriff. Slade nodded.

"But he ran up against a snag," Slade resumed. "The small landowner, especially the Texas-Mexican, who are in the majority, wouldn't sell even at what looked to be a fair price. They are deeply rooted here. Many of their relatives live in Nuevo Laredo or its environs. They intermarry across the river and share their social activities. So Danver brought in Brandon and his bunch, took a little local talent in tow and formed his Land Committee with Brandon as the front. Then he began a campaign of intimidation. The law, with its intricate maneuvers, has a terror for such people. When their titles, some of which are necessarily vague, were questioned and it was subtly intimated that they were no good, a lot of them got scared and sold out. The stubborn ones were intimidated by physical violence. Several of the more stubborn who didn't scare easily, like Sebastian Telo, were murdered. That part of the groundwork was Brandon's chore, and I've a notion Brandon sort of got out of hand, like in the whipping of Felipe Cardena. He was naturally a sadistic, cruel devil and enjoyed his role of chief executioner for the Land Committee."

"One thing to Danver's credit, sticking a knife through the wind spider's neck," grunted Medford.

"Yes, but there he made my case against him," Slade said. "I knew at once that Danver killed Brandon. I knew he realized that Brandon was responsible for the attempt against his life that night in The Montezuma."

"And you saved the sidewinder's life for him," growled Medford.

"Yes," Slade agreed, "but he's not the sort to appreciate it. He's perfectly willing to do me in if he can."

"A snake-blooded hellion for fair," said Medford. "But there's one thing I don't understand: Why did he take the Pablo Navarez case and win it against the committee."

"That was for show," Slade explained. "To make it appear he is an impartial attorney who takes clients where he can find them and has no personal interest in their activities. The Land Committee never wanted the Navarez holding; it would be of no value to them. And it was necessary that Danver's connections with the committee not be known. It was a clever move on his part.

"But," he added thoughtfully, "I think Danver slipped bad when he enlisted the support of Ralpho Flores. He thought that by so doing he could induce Flores to pull something that would crystallize public opinion against the valley landowners. Smart enough, except he can't control Flores, which, in my opinion, he is beginning to realize. Nobody can control Flores, who is a born revolutionary as well as being a natural bandido."

"Right on both counts," nodded the sheriff.

"There's a strange quirk in that little jigger's makeup," Slade remarked, his eyes laughing. "His passionate love of music. He's utterly ruthless, but I've a notion he'd hesitate to harm me personally just because I can sing, after a fashion."

"After a fashion!" snorted Medford. "You could make a fortune in grand opry."

"You're prejudiced, and, no doubt, a little tone deaf," Slade smiled. "But to get back to serious things, Flores has me worried. I've not the least notion what he has in mind, but it's something."

"Something we won't like," predicted Medford. "After what you heard last night, are you going to drop a loop on Danver?" Slade shook his head.

"Not enough evidence. It would be my word against Danver, and that isn't sufficient."

"Your prestige as a Texas Ranger should count for something."

"Yes, but our system of jurisprudence maintains that a man is innocent until proven guilty, beyond a reasonable doubt. A good lawyer could raise all sorts of 'reasonable doubts,' especially with Wilton Danver to coach him. I'll have to have something more definite on Danver before I make my throw."

"Meanwhile he's running around loose and very likely figuring another try at doing you in," the sheriff said in exasperated tones.

Slade shrugged his broad. shoulders. "Could be," he conceded. "What I'm more bothered about is what Ralpho Flores has in mind. I'm confident Danver is going to slip, sooner or later, and give us all we need to hogtie him."

"Wonder where the hellion got the notion for his scheme in the first place?" observed Medford.

"Hard to tell," Slade replied. "He may have read or heard about a similar procedure that was put into effect down around Brownsville years ago. That one backfired, too, but not until after a lot of folks had been killed, and a general hell-raising that's still talked about. I hope to prevent a reoccurrence here. The spade work has already been done to create such a condition."

- Regarding his sternly composed countenance, Sheriff Medford thought it was typical of Walt Slade to subserviate his own very real personal danger to his concern for others.

"I'm keeping a close watch on Nuevo Laredo," Slade observed. "A lot of bitterness building up over there and in the surrounding country. Some of the folks who were driven out of the valley are living over there with friends or relatives and the stories they have to tell are inflammatory, to say the least. It's a powder keg."

"Some of those wild young hellions down there could make trouble, all right," Medford agreed. "Liable not to be safe for folks here to cross the bridge. And there's quite a few who work there, just as quite a few Nuevo Laredo folks work here. Always been the friendliest relations between the two towns until of late. Now relations are getting a mite strained."

"That's the worst of such things," Slade commented. "Sooner or later innocent people are embroiled." The sheriff nodded sober agreement.

"By the way," he said, "nobody reported seeing a body down there by Zaragoza Street; that's funny."

"Not too surprising," Slade said. "Chances are it was chucked in the river by the other hellions who didn't care to have it found. Somewhere in the Gulf of Mexico by now, the chances are. Do you happen to be acquainted with anybody by the name of Johnson? I have reason to believe that was the fellow's name."

"Johnson," the sheriff repeated. "There's a Hi Johnson who runs a saloon over on Bruni Street. Say! That's one of the saloon owners mixed up with the Land Committee."

"Was mixed up with the Land Committee," Slade corrected grimly. "Suppose you amble over to his place and casually ask for him. I'm quite anxious to know if he's still around. I'll wait for you here."

"Okay," replied Medford, and left the office. Slade rolled a cigarette and settled himself comfortably in his chair.

Less than half an hour passed before the sheriff returned.

"Not there," he announced. "I asked the day bartender where I might find him. Said he hadn't any notion, that he hadn't been seen since late last night. Heard he left before closing time and hadn't shown up since, although he most always came in shortly after noon. Jigger seemed a mite puzzled. Said he'd stay on and wait for him if he hadn't showed before his relief came on."

"I've a notion he'll have a darned long wait," Slade said. "Was Johnson a big man?"

"Pretty husky," the sheriff replied. "Not as tall as you but even broader. I recall hearing once that he used to be a professional wrestler."

"I can well believe it," Slade conceded. "Rather fast with a gun, too."

"Most of those old-time saloon owners are," nodded the sheriff. "They sometimes need to be. Yep, I believe the jigger you downed was Johnson, all right. Seems I've heard too, that he was something of a knife man; used to practice throwing in the back room."

"It's beginning to tie up," Slade said. "But there's still too much slack in the twine. Who's the other saloon owner who is a member of the Land Committee? I don't recall his name. The one on San Agustin Avenue."

"Doty," replied the sheriff. "Mort Doty."

"Mort?" Slade repeated. "Mort—Martin. It is tieing up." He rose to his feet. "I think I'll have a look at Senor Doty," he said.

Slade had no difficulty locating the saloon on San Agustin Avenue, which had "Doty's Place" legended across the window. He strolled in and ordered a drink.

Standing at the far end of the bar was a hatchet-faced man whom he instantly recognized as the argumentive Martin of the night before. He noted that Doty appeared ill at ease under his scrutiny. However, he did not leave his place at the end of the bar and after a single glance ignored the ranger. Slade finished his drink and walked out. A sidewise glance at the back bar mirror showed Doty's gaze following him to the door.

" 'The guilty flee when no man pursueth,' " he quoted. "Senor Doty has the jitters."

19

THE RANCHERO WAS a flat-bottomed old tub, devoid of paint or dignity. But her hull was sturdy and sound, her engines excellent. Her massive paddles beat the muddy water of the swollen Rio Grande with resounding slaps, announcing her contempt for old debbil river at its worst. Glints of star reflections sparkled up around her blunt bow. Her wake was a tossing band of phosporescent moonlight.

Disregarding the current, she plowed steadily ahead, her exhaust "chow-chowing" with explosive monotony. For years she had been making the trip between Brownsville and Laredo and back, her hold crammed with merchandise. She'd had plenty of adventures in her day, but she didn't talk about them.

She carried a cargo of sugar, coffee, kerosene and other odds and ends. Most of the oil was in barrels and cans stacked on her afterdeck.

In the captain's cabin stood a ponderous iron safe. Like the Ranchero, it was ancient, and like the Ranchero, it did not look particularly prosperous. But in that safe was a very large sum of money consigned to a Laredo bank.

The safe door stood open, for it also contained invoices and other papers over which the captain worked at his table-desk bolted to a bulkhead.

In the deck house Alf Higgins, the pilot, lounged comfortably against the wheel, casting an occasional glance at the dark loom of the nearby bank, for here the channel ran close to the Mexican shore. Higgins knew that channel as well as he knew the paths of his own backyard. There were no rocks or other obstructions. All he had to do was hold her nose straight and keep watch for a possible drifting log or drowned steer borne on the crest of the flood. The spokes hardly moved in his gnarled hands.

The Ranchero carried a big crew, mostly roustabouts adept at wrestling bales and boxes. Some were sleeping on the deck, others squatting in groups, talking. They were a hard lot, ready for anything. Now they looked forward to Laredo's waterfront saloons with the anticipation that is often more pleasurable than realization. Low laughter welled up, and the muted murmur of low voices. Everything was peaceful on the *Ranchero*, peaceful as the hush of the night.

Alf Higgins gazed ahead, saw nothing but the star-dimpled water flowing smoothly and steadily toward the cleaving bow. His eyelids drooped sleepily.

The next instant he was stretched on the deck, his ears ringing with the tremendous crash that split the silence wide open. The *Ranchero* shivered from stem to stern, bucked back like an angry horse, surged forward, and struck again. The pound of her exhaust snapped off. Her paddles hung dripping and swaying idly. She lurched, tossed, swung crazily toward the shore. Yelps and curses arose as the knocked-down crewmen scrambled to their feet, sprawling and spraddling on the slanting deck.

Over the rail swarmed a score of masked men, a small, upright figure in the lead.

'Surrender!" he shouted. "You're covered!"

But the captain was a salty oldtimer who had had experience with river pirates before and was not one to be pushed around with impunity. He commenced banging away with an old Smith & Wesson forty-five. The next moment, he died, two bullets laced through his heart. Alf Higgins peered from the wheelhouse and got a slug through the shoulder.

But now the crewmen, ensconced behind bales and boxes, were fighting back. A battle royal ensued. Curses in two languages and the bellowing of the guns quivered the air. The *Ranchero* bumped and slithered against the high bank.

The small leader of the pirates darted into the captain's cabin, two of his men crowding on his heels. Swiftly they looted the safe, stuffing the packets of bills and the rolls of gold coin into canvas sacks. On the deck the battle still raged, with not too many casualties on either side, for a thick cloud had drifted over the moon and the night was black as pitch.

Suddenly there was a flicker of flame which spread with amazing rapidity. Bullets had punctured the barrels and cans of kerosene and the oil was flooding over the deck.

An instant later there was a thunderous explosion. Blazing cans of oil skyrocketed through the air. In seconds the whole after part of the Ranchero was a seething inferno.

The fighting ceased. The pirates streamed back over the rail, except for several that lay sprawled on the burning deck. The crewmen, what was left of them, dived into the water to escape the flames and swam frantically for the shore. Through the darkness sounded the beat of fast hoofs fading away into the south.

Most of the crew made it to the shore. A brawny Swede who could swim like a porpoise towed the wounded Alf Higgins to safety. For a while they lay catching their breath, the Swede working over Higgins the while.

"Where the devil are we?" the Swede asked.

"About ten miles below Laredo, I'd say," replied Higgins who, his shoulder padded and bandaged with strips torn from shirts, puffed on a cigarette manufactured from tobacco and paper that had escaped a wetting in a waterproof pouch. "It's going to be a darned long walk."

"It'll be hard on you, Alf," someone remarked.

"I'll make it," declared the indomitable Higgins. "The blasted thing went through low down and to the side; no bones busted. And I don't walk on my hands. The poor old skipper; he didn't have a chance, and we're seven more short." He burst forth with a flood of appalling profanity, his companions ably abetting him.

"But cussin' won't help matters," he said. "If you fellers have caught your breath, we'd better be moving. Ain't good to lay around in wet clothes; walking will dry 'em. Thank Pete, the night's warm."

"Who were those hellions who jumped us?" wondered the Swede. "Think they were Mexicans?"

"Wouldn't be surprised if some of 'em were," replied Higgins, getting painfully to his feet. "I heard a lot of Spanish cussin', but the runt who 'peared to be giving the orders sure spoke good English. Sidewinders from both sides of the river, the chances are. Don't matter, you find skunks everywhere. Let's get going."

It was full daylight when the bedraggled and footsore survivors limped across the bridge and reported the outrage. The waterfront seethed and Laredo was filled with wild conjecture as to who were the perpetrators.

"Well, guess we know now what Flores had in mind," Sheriff Medford observed to Slade.

The ranger shook his head. "Don't think so," he replied. "No, that wasn't it. That was just a typical *bandido* raid engineered with unusual skill. We don't even know if Flores was responsible. The crew said a short man appeared to be giving the orders, but there are lots of short men on both sides of the river."

"What I'd like to know is how the devil did the hellions know the money was on that old tub," said Medford. "It was supposed to be a closely guarded secret, the bank people told me. The shipment was sent by water because they figured it was safer than by stage from Brownsville."

"I've a notion the hand of our *amigo* Danver shows there," Slade replied dryly. "I understand he is quite friendly with the bank people. He got it out of somebody and passed it on to somebody else, presumably Flores. Sort of payment in advance, as it were."

"Blast it! Payment for what?" exploded the sheriff.

"That's what we still don't know," Slade returned.

The sheriff swore. "Well, what are we going to do about it?" he demanded.

"There's nothing we can do about it," Slade replied. "By the terms of the treaty of Guadalupe-Hidalgo, the Rio Grande is the boundary and it happened on the Mexican side. It's up to the Mexican authorities. We have no authority down there.

"But I would like to ride down there and look things over," he added. "I'd like to find out what wrecked the *Ranchero*. The pilot swears there are no rocks in the channel and never have been, and he should know. I understand he's made the trip a hundred times. But he said what happened was just what would have happened had the boat struck a submerged ledge. I've a notion how it was done, but I'd like to make sure. If I'm right, it was something you'd hardly expect from a band of Mexican raiders. What do you say? We've got plenty of time to make it before dark."

"All right," grunted the sheriff. "A breath of fresh air won't hurt. This darn town's stuffy."

"You're right," Slade agreed. "And Shadow needs to stretch his legs. He's getting almighty tired of being cooped up. Gave me a look this morning that said he was ready to take my head off if I didn't do something about it soon."

"I figure he's capable of doing just that," chuckled the sheriff. "Let's go."

They had no trouble locating the point where the robbery occurred. The hulk of the *Ranchero*, burned down to the water's edge, lay grounded on the south bank. Slade spared the wreck hardly a glance. Turning Shadow, he rode slowly back up the river, studying the swift water. He drew rein opposite where a persistent riffle broke the otherwise smooth surface of the river.

"There it is," he said. "And mighty smart work, too. They built cribbing in mid-channel and filled it with stones. Must have done most of the work before the river began to rise and the water here was shallow. When the river is low, the channel is farther out toward midstream. Somebody with plenty of savvy studied the river and figured it out. I don't consider Flores capable of that. *Amigo* Danver again, I'll wager."

"That hellion is a devil," declared the sheriff.

"Yes, in more ways than one," Slade agreed. "Let's go home."

Slade enjoyed the ride, part of which was under the stars. They arrived at Laredo ravenously hungry and proceeded to The Montezuma to take care of that.

The wrecking of the *Ranchero* and the murder of her captain and crew members was the chief topic of conversation in The Montezuma. Men gestured with flushed and angry faces, going over the lurid details again and again. Fists pounded the bar, fierce wrangles broke out here and there, and some isolated indulgences in personalities. There was little fundamental difference of opinion, however.

Slade listened intently to the discussions that raged on every side, and arrived at a conclusion.

"You'll notice there is no intimation that the valley dwellers might be directly or indirectly responsible," he observed to the sheriff in low tones. "They are never mentioned. Which tends to corroborate my contention that the piracy was not what Danver insinuated into Flores' mind."

"Looks like you're right," admitted the sheriff. "A pity

we couldn't find any bodies down there; they might have told us something."

"Burned up or washed away," Slade said. "That's why I didn't do any searching to amount to anything. It was a foregone conclusion that we wouldn't discover them. Chances are it wouldn't have meant much if we had. Flores enlists his men from everywhere, and he has plenty to draw from. He'd be smart enough to use only strangers to this section, I imagine. So that nothing could be tied to him. Nobody ever has been able to get anything on Flores or prove anything against him. He's shrewd, but he's also impulsive. He may fly off the handle because of something and give us the lead we need. That's one of the things I'm hoping for. Danver is different. He's cold, calculating, and explores all the angles before he acts. But I still believe that in Flores he's got something he can't control. That's what I'm expecting to give us our big break, perhaps in some manner totally unforeseen by Danver and which he won't be able to take precautions against. There's always a weak spot in an outlaw's armor which eventually proves his undoing. Danver saw opportunity in the person of Ralpho Flores, and perhaps in his eagerness to grasp that oportunity, overlooked the imponderable which is the character of Ralpho Flores. Anyhow, that's what I'm hoping."

"And Flores may have made a mistake in trusting Danver," the sheriff commented.

"Yes," Slade agreed. "Danver will doublecross him if he considers it expedient to do so. But men of action like Flores, are not to be trifled with. Danver is playing with dynamite if he plans to cut the ground from under Flores."

"And I hope it blows up in his face, the snake-blooded horned toad!" growled Medford. "Lok, there's the side-winder now!"

Wilton Danver paused just inside the door and glanced around. He waved a genial greeting, smiled and nodded and sauntered to the bar. The sheriff swore.

"That grin of his is too blasted smug," he said, still growling. "He figures he's got us where the hair is short."

"As a matter of fact, he has, at the moment," Slade said. "Right now he can afford to grin. He must have gotten his cut of that sixty thousand dollar haul and figures to keep it. That's something I learned about Flores; he's meticulously honest with those who work for and with him. Everybody gets his allotted share, with no favorites played. He's something of an anomaly of his kind."

"A sort of modern Robin Hood, eh?" grunted the sheriff. "Steal from the rich and give to the poor."

"Yes, but with one fundamental difference; Flores doesn't give a darn whom he steals from, just so he steals."

The sheriff's leathery countenance split in a grin. "You have the darndest way of saying things, but even when I don't know what the devil you're talking about, it makes sense."

Slade smiled and took the paradoxical compliment as it was meant.

Wilton Danver finished his drink, chatted a few minutes with the bartender and departed. At the door, he again waved airily to Slade and the sheriff, smiled and nodded.

Medford turned red with anger. "The blankety-blank-blank is pokin' fun at us," he declared.

"Don't worry, we may have the last laugh," Slade counseled.

Cradlebaugh, the Land Office investigator, dropped in. "Well, I had another talk with Judge Parkinson," he said as he accepted a drink. "Wasn't as tractable as he was last time. Was almost combative. Vigorously defended his original handling of the Telo case. Insisted that he acted in good faith. That he had no reason to believe that the letter presumably written by Sebastian Telo to Pablo Navarez was a forgery. Maintained that he had never seen a specimen of Telo's handwriting and that none was brought forward. And that he also had no reason to think that the testimony of Navarez and the other two witnesses was perjured. Somebody had put some stiffening in his backbone, I'd say.

"But I did get this much. The heirs of Sebastian Telo may reoccupy the property whenever they are of a mind to. Parkinson is reversing his ruling in the face of fresh testimony. He's not waiting for the Land Office to crack down on him. Which is wise on his part. Something else might come out that he wouldn't find palatable. He appeared to get a bit nervous when I expressed the opinion that Sebastian Telo was murdered to prevent him from appealing the case. When I casually mentioned that if a murder was proven against somebody, that some other people might find themselves facing charges of accessory after the fact, he seemed downright jumpy. I've a notion he may know more, or suspect more, about Telo's death than he would care to admit."

"Very likely," Slade said, "but he strikes me as being a slippery old coot who always manages to stay just inside the law. Will very likely be hard to get anything on him. By the way, I believe Telo's herd of cows is still on the property?"

"That's right," replied Cradlebaugh. "The Land Committe hired a caretaker and a couple of assistants to look after the stock." He drew forth a legal looking document.

"Here's an order directing them to vacate at once," he told Medford. "Have one of your deputies serve it tomorrow, please. You know the heirs, don't you?" The sheriff nodded.

"Notify them of the reversed ruling, will you? I imagine they'll want to take over without delay."

"Guess Slade will handle that chore for us," replied the sheriff, smiling broadly.

"I'll be plumb pleased to," Slade promised, also smiling.

Cradlebaugh finished his drink and the sheriff instantly ordered another. The investigator nodded his appreciation.

"I'm going to keep on digging," he said. "Sooner or later, I'll get to the bottom of this smelly mess and, I hope, tie something onto the rest of those rascals. That is, if you gentlemen don't beat me to it with something more serious."

"We're not having much luck so far," Slade admitted.

"Anyhow, from what I gather, you're thinning them out a bit," said Cradlebaugh.

"But the head's still loose, and until we pin that in a forked stick we haven't accomplished much," Slade replied.

"You'll do it, I have every faith in you," Cradlebaugh insisted. "No, no more to drink; I'm going to bed."

"That young feller's a go-getter," commented the sheriff. "Old Parkinson had beter look out. He's got his eye on him and if that spavined coot has anything to hide he'll turn it up, see if he don't."

Slade nodded and rolled a cigarette. He'd formed a similar opinion of John Cradlebaugh.

A man pushed through the swinging doors, glanced about searchingly and spotted the sheriff. He hurried to the table. It was the head bartender at Hi Johnson's saloon on Bruni Street.

"Tobe," he said without preamble, "I'm worried. Johnson hasn't showed up yet. Nobody's seen hair or hide of him. Beginning to look like it might be a chore for you. I'm afraid something has happened to him."

"Okay, I'll look into it," replied the sheriff. "Let me know if he shows up."

"I will," the bartender promised. Looking somewhat relieved, he hurried out.

"Yep, something happened to him, all right, the blasted vinegaroon," the sheriff observed dryly. "He was the hellion who tried to knife you, no doubt of it. Well, that makes two prominent members of the Land Committee among the missing. And a few small fry. We ain't doing too bad. And I reckon the little Telo gal will be mighty pleased to get her home back."

"Yes, she will be," Slade agreed. "And that's going to be a very valuable holding before long. It's the best land in the valley."

"Uh-huh," nodded the sheriff, and added with apparent irrelevance, "Nice gal, nice holding. That's a combination that should interest any young feller who ought to be thinking of settling down."

Slade smiled, but did not comment.

But he looked forward with pleasure to the meeting with Marie later that night. He hadn't forgotten the tears in her beautiful dark eyes as she gazed at the little white ranchhouse where she was born and spent her happy girlhood. Yes, he would greatly enjoy meeting Marie tonight, even more than usual.

20

HE WAS TO MEET HER sooner than he anticipated. When he and Sheriff Medford returned to the office they found a dainty feminine figure perched in the sheriff's chair, shapely legs comfortably crossed.

"She won't go away!" wailed the deputy in charge of the office during the sheriff's absence. "Not that I really wanted her to," he added. "But it just ain't the place for a nice gal this time of night."

"Marie!" Slade exclaimed. "What in blazes are you doing here?"

"Waiting for you," she replied composedly. "Listen, Walt, there's going to be trouble."

"Trouble?"

"Yes. Estaban brought me the word and told me to find you as quickly as possible. I figured you'd be here so I came and waited. I was just going to send this nice deputy looking for you. Walt, you know Estaban has been watching Ralpho Flores—he hates him—and listening to everything he could hear. Tonight he learned something. Flores is going to raid the town tonight. He is already on this side of the river, he and more than fifty of his men. They are lying hidden in a house down on Zaragoza Street. The house, Estaban said, where Cale Brandon was found killed. Estaban said you'd know where it is. Flores plans to wait until people are asleep, then he will strike. He'll kill and burn and loot. He says that the mistreated people of the valley must be avenged and receive justice, but Estaban says what he is after is loot."

"Estaban is right," Slade replied grimly. "Honey, you and Estaban have done everybody a good chore tonight. If it wasn't for you, the hellions would have gotten away with it."

Sheriff Medford was swearing steadily under his mustache. "We'll fix the sidewinders," he said. "I'll get a posse together and we'll go down there and blow them from under their hats."

Slade shook his head. "Won't do," he replied. "If we go

133

134   GUNSMOKE ON THE RIO GRANDE

barging down there, no matter how many of us, we'll be the ones that'll get blown from under our hats. And you haven't got time to assemble a big posse of dependable men; it's already past midnight. Trust Flores to be keeping a watch for just such a contingency. It'll mean a lot of people getting killed, and I want to avoid that if possible."

"Estaban said there are guards posted and keeping an eye on the town," Marie interpolated.

"Does that hellion believe he can get away with it!" raved the sheriff.

"He does, and he will, if he isn't stopped," Slade replied grimly. "Remember what happened in Brownsville, a lot bigger town than this. Cheno Cortinas with less than a hundred men took complete possession of Brownsville, killed a number of people, looted and burned and held the town until he got good and ready to leave, more than forty-eight hours later. A sorry spectacle that, an American city of several thousand people occupied and held in thrall by a bunch of bandits. We don't want a repeat here. Let me think a minute."

They watched him expectantly as he stood with knitted brows.

"I believe I've got it," he said at length. "You know the old Indian Crossing at the river end of Bruni Street? We'll cross there, slip back across the bridge and take the hellions from the rear. We'll be all over them before they know what's hit them. They may even surrender without firing a shot, although I consider that unlikely."

The sheriff looked decidedly startled. "But the river's mighty high and that crossing is treacherous even during low water, especially if you don't know just how the ledge runs. One misstep and you tumble off and are pounded to pieces in no time. And I don't know of anybody who's ever crossed it."

Marie stood up. "I'll guide you across," she said. "I've waded it a number of times and know the ledge by heart."

"You will not, it's too dangerous," Slade declared.

Marie's little rounded white chin went up. "I will!" she declared, just as positively. "Listen, Walt Slade, don't start telling me what I shall do and what I shan't do. I have a mind of my own. I'm going to guide you across, and that's all there is to it."

Despite the seriousness of the moment, the sheriff raised

a hand to his mustache to hide a grin. The deputy didn't
bother to hide his and chuckled out loud. Walt Slade was
not given to theatrical gestures of any kind, but now he
shook both fists in the air and swore, under his breath.

"Women!" he exploded. "When you get mixed up with
them, your troubles begin."

Marie slanted him a glance through her lashes. A dimple showed beside her red mouth.

"And don't you love it!" she said softly.

"I won't love it if you get drowned," he growled.

"I won't get drowned," she replied cheerfully. "And if
you clumsy men will just follow me carefully and step
where I step, nobody will get drowned. How soon can we
start?"

Slade gave up. "All right," he said. "Medford, get your
posse together as fast as you can. Twenty-five should be
enough. Work fast but carefully. Choose only men who
can keep their mouths shut and not alarm the town. That
would give the whole thing away and they'd be ready for
us."

"Okay," said the sheriff. "Come on, Sime." He and the
deputy hurried out. Slade sat down and recounted what
Cradlebaugh told him relative to the Telo land.

Again there were tears in Marie's eyes, but this time
they were tears of gladness.

"It will be wonderful to be home," she breathed.
"Won't it, Walt?"

And Walt Slade unhesitatingly answered, "Yes."

Soon men began filing into the closely shuttered office,
grim, purposeful men armed with rifles and six-guns. They
kept coming until there were twenty-three of them in all.
The sheriff and the deputy arrived.

"All I could risk," he told Slade.

"Should be enough," the ranger replied. "Slip out one
at a time. We'll meet just north of the river end of Bruni
Street, at the crossing. Come on, Marie, we'll go first."

Marie slipped on the dark cloak that covered her scanty
dance floor costume and together they hurried out. It was
already very late and there were only a few stragglers on
the street, who paid them no mind. They reached the
point of rendezvous and waited. Soon the whole posse was
assembled. At their feet the river moaned and muttered.

A line of ripples, faintly outlined in the light of the dying moon, showed the course of the dangerous crossing.

Marie threw off her cloak. "Walt, you follow next to me, with a hand on my shoulder," she ordered. "Sheriff you keep a hand on his shoulder, the next man with a hand on yours. That way you won't get out of line. Step carefully and don't hurry. Ready? Let's go!"

She stepped fearlessly into the water that frothed and bubbled about her ankles and rose higher and higher until she was leaning upstream against the force of the current Slade followed close, his grip tight on her slim shoulder. If she went over the edge into the raging whirlpool below the ledge they would go together.

Unhurriedly but without hesitation, she led the way, her little feet treading firmly on the uneven surface of the sunken ledge, as gracefully as they tripped across the dance floor. Gracefully, and without fear.

"If we'd had some generals like her during the War, we wouldn't have lost it," a lanky Texan behind the sheriff remarked audibly.

They reached the middle of the river, where the current ran fiercest, for here the channel was almost midstream. Marie's slender body bent like a reed against the pound of the water. Once or twice she stumbled slightly on the uneven surface of the ledge and Slade's grip on her shoulder tightened till she winced; he was taking no chances of her slipping from his grasp. On either side the whirlpools stormed and raved, gnawing in baffled fury against the stubborn stone. Behind him Sheriff Medford grumbled curses. The possemen muttered apprehensively.

"I like fish and I've et a mighty lot of 'em," sighed the lank Texan. "So I guess it's only fair that the fish cat me."

"If they do, they'll have less brains in their bellies than they've got in their heads," grunted the sheriff. "The blasted bank over there don't seem to get any closer."

It did, however, and eventually they reached it, stepping onto firm ground with sighs of relief.

"I don't want to go through that again, even following the trail of a pretty woman," declared the sheriff, mopping his brow. "A couple of times I thought I was a goner. You wouldn't live minutes in that devil's cauldron below the ledge. Now what?"

"To the bridge and slip across quietly," Slade said. "I

don't think there'll be a guard posted there. They won't expect any interruption from this side of the river." He turned to Marie.

"I'm not going to order you to, but please go home now and wait there until it's all over. You've done your chore, wonderfully, but please don't make things harder for me by causing me to worry about you."

"Very well," she replied, "I'll—wait. But please come to me as soon as you can."

"I will," he promised and watched her walk south, her shoulders drooping a little.

"Poor gal!" muttered the sheriff. "Waiting is harder than fighting. Let's go, fellers."

Silently as ghosts they stole across the bridge, meeting with no untoward incident. In the dark hour before the dawn Laredo lay sleeping. Everything appeared calm and peaceful with no intimation that at any moment the night might erupt in violence and death.

"We'll slide up that alley beside the building and wait there," Slade said. "Highly unlikely that the alley will be guarded. They'll be keeping watch on the town and not give this direction any thought. Careful, now, and don't make the slightest noise. We won't make a move until they are assembled outside the building and ready to rush the town. Then we'll crack down on them. Medford, you do the talking."

"What we oughta do," somebody grumbled, "is cut loose on the devils as soon as they're bunched."

Slade shook his head. "We are peace officers and must conduct ourselves as peace officers. I know it lessens our advantage, but we have to give them a chance to surrender. And if they happen to realize the jig is up and don't fight back, very likely lives will be saved."

"Makes sense," grunted the sheriff. "Anyhow, that's the way we're going to handle it. But if you see a single move after I give them their chance, cut loose on 'em with everything you've got."

"If it comes to shooting, shoot straight and shoot fast," Slade added. "Don't forget, we're Texans with the reputation of hitting what we aim at. It's up to us to live up to our reputation. We'd better! All right, the alley is over this way. Let's go."

They glided into the alley. One man was left to guard

the bridge head against a possible attempt to escape by some of the raiders. Where the narrow lane opened onto Zaragoza Street they paused, keeping well back in the gloom, but where they could view the street.

The street was deserted, and utterly silent. No sound broke the stillness except the murmur of the distant river that was loud in the great hush. Nowhere was there a gleam of light or any hint of movement. The slice of moon, now higher in the heavens, filtered a wan glow that reflected from the uneven cobbles.

"Maybe the hellions have already left and are headed into the town," Medford breathed nervously to Slade.

"I don't think so," the ranger whispered back. "Just about now would be the time to move. Take it easy and keep your eyes skinned and your ears open."

A tedious and nerve-wracking fifteen minutes passed. Slade glanced at the eastern sky, anticipating the first faint graying of the coming dawn. Now he himself was growing a bit anxious; the dead silence and the absolute lack of movement was depressing.

A sound broke the silence, the sound of a voice speaking in very low tones. The posse tensed; hands tightened their grips on rifles. Nobody hardly dared breathe.

Shadowy forms appeared in the street, apparently materializing from nowhere; but Slade knew they were slipping from the dark hallway where Cale Brandon met his death. Like evil spirits rising from unblessed graves they loomed in the darkness. Slade could just make out a tall and broad-shouldered figure towering above the others.

"Danver!" he breathed. "But I don't see Flores. All set? They're clumping together. I think that's all of them. Okay, Medford."

The sheriff took a long stride forward, the posse surging behind him. His voice blared forth, shattering the silence.

"Elevate! You're covered! In the name of the State of Texas, you are under arrest!"

The bandits whirled in the direction of the sound, staring with dilated eyes at the leveled rifles. For a moment it seemed the coup was completely succesful, that they would offer no resistance.

Then suddenly there was movement among their ranks. Flame gushed, a posseman cried out as the bullet went

home. Instantly the street exploded in flame and smoke
and thundering sound.

Curses, yells of rage, screams of agony blended with the
staccato booming of the guns. Slade got a glimpse of
Wilton Danver but instantly lost him in the swirling
smoke and the confusion of movement. As he moved forward, shooting with both hands, he thought he saw a
shadow flicker in the dark mouth of the alley across the
street but couldn't be sure, and he only had a fleeting
glance to spare; the pitched battle was still raging as the
bandits, caught off balance, demoralized though they
were, fought back with the recklessness of despair as the
rifles took their fearful toll.

Abruptly it was over. The street was littered with bodies.
Those of the bandits who remained alive were throwing
down their weapons and howling for mercy. Slade's voice
rolled out as thunder to stop the shooting. Silence descended again, broken by the moans and cries of the
wounded and dying.

Then suddenly a clatter of hoofs sounded down the
street.

"There goes Flores!" yelled the sheriff. "He had a
horse!"

Slade threw up his gun, but before he could line sights
the bandit leader had whisked around the corner and
vanished. A moment later a single shot sounded from the
direction of the bridge.

"Either Silas got him or he got Silas," said Medford.

Slade listened intently.

"Hoofbeats on the floor boards of the bridge," he said.
"Looks like he got Silas. Send somebody over there in a
hurry. Is Danver among that bunch?"

Together they peered into the faces of the sullen pris-
oners, examined the bodies on the ground.

"Not here," said the sheriff. "Now where did the hellion
get to?"

"Maybe he got across the bridge on foot," Slade guessed.
"Come on, let's get over there. If Silas isn't dead maybe
he can tell us."

They raced to the bridgehead and found the posseman
who had been sent to investigate was trying to care for
Silas's bullet-punctured shoulder.

"Nobody but Flores went across," Silas declared, volleying oaths. "He was on top of me before I knew it. I hadn't figured on anybody on horseback and held my fire till too late. He plugged me and kept on going."

"Nothing to do about *him*," Slade said, "but Danver—"

"We'll get the horned toad," declared the sheriff. "We'll comb the town like a chaparral brake. He can't get away."

"I'm not so sure," Slade replied. "He'll head for Mexico, the only place he'll be safe. Medford, I think I've got it, and I'm going to try and cut him off. You look after things here. Did we lose many?"

"Three dead, half a dozen wounded, only two seriously," replied the sheriff. "We did for nigh onto twenty of those hellions. I'll take care of 'em, all right. Where you going?"

"To Bruni Street," Slade flung over his shoulder as he trotted north on San Bernardo Avenue.

He took it easy at first, gradually increasing his pace. He had more than two miles to cover before reaching the river end of Bruni Street, and he would need all he had. He was playing a hunch that the wily Danver would try to make it to Mexico and safety by way of the Indian Crossing. The flicker of shadow he had noted in the north mouth of the alley was Wilton Danver sneaking out of the fight, intent only on saving his own hide. And he might well succeed. Slade hoped the lawyer would pause at his office for money or something long enough to allow his pursuer to reach the Crossing first. He steadily increased his gait until he was running at top speed, head bent, elbows pressed against his sides. He was in excellent physical condition, but before long his heart was pounding, his breath coming unevenly.

Heads were sticking out of windows, now, shouting questions that Slade didn't take time to answer. Nobody was venturing into the street. The row on the waterfront must have sounded like the Battle of Antietam to the citizens of Laredo.

The east was graying and soon the dawn would break. Be good shooting light, he told himself grimly and sped doggedly on.

He reached Bruni Street after what seemed an eternity of agonizing effort. More than half the way covered, now, but still plenty to go. He eased up for a few minutes, caught his second wind and raced ahead. Now in the strengthening light he could see the gleam of the river although it seemed miles and miles distant. He knew he was nearing physical exhaustion. His legs were trembling a bit, his gait a trifle unsteady. Once he stumbled from sheer weariness for there was nothing to stumble over. His eyes felt as if they were trying to burst from their sockets. There was a salt taste of blood in his mouth and he realized that his teeth were biting into his lower lip.

He reached the end of the street, swerved north and the Indian Crossing was before him.

And near the middle of the river, sloshing through the shallow water that flowed over the ledge, a tall figure forged steadily toward the distant Mexican shore.

Because he had to, Slade paused a couple of minutes to catch his breath, then stepped onto the Crossing, striding over the uneven surface as swiftly as he dared. He knew very well the odds were against him. Unless he managed to get close enough to bring Danver down with a lucky shot, the lawyer would reach Mexico and find sanctuary where Slade had no authority to search him out.

The crossing had been bad enough earlier in the night when he was fresh and there was no need to hurry, and with a guide who was familiar with the treacherous reef. Now, nearly prostrated with fatigue, his steps uncertain and with the need for speed urgent, it was an agonizing trudge with death reaching for him every foot of the way.

He was gaining a bit, for Danver was not having it too easy, either. His hand dropped to his holster, fell away. The distance was too great, his eyes were blurred, his hands shaking. He had to get a little closer. The numbness of failure was coiling about his heart, but with grim perseverance he strode on, paying scant attention to where he set his feet, intent only on the form ahead.

Danver reached the far shore, clambered onto firm ground. Slade's hand again dropped to his gun butt. Danver was now on Mexican soil, but he would make one last try at stopping him.

From behind a boulder leaped a small, upright figure. Ralpho Flores' screaming voice came clearly over the water.

"You doublecrossed me, you crawling skunk! You set a trap for me!"

Slade saw the two hands flicker. He saw the orange flashes, pale in the strengthening light, gush back and forth. He saw Flores reel, steady himself for a last shot, and fall to lie motionless.

Wilton Danver took a step forward, another, his feet dragging, staggering drunkenly. One more faltering step. He reached Flores' body and plunged onto his face. In the pale light the two forms made a great cross on the ground.

Wearily, Slade trudged on till he reached the shore and managed to crawl up the bank. He lurched to where the two forms lay. Flores was dead, but Danver's shoulders twitched a little. Slade knelt beside him and turned him over on his back. Danver gazed up at him with glazing eyes. Words seeped past the blood frothing his lips.

"You—win! I don't—know—what you hope to make—of it—but—you win!"

"No, Danver, I don't win," Slade replied. "Law and justice wins." He held the star of the rangers before the dying man's eyes.

"They told—me—in Texas—the—the rangers would—get me!" Danver gasped. "They—did!"

The symbol of law and order and justice for even the most lowly was the last thing he looked upon on this earth.

Slade rose to his feet, gazed down at the two motionless forms. Then he staggered away from the river. Maybe he had enough left to make it to the home of Estaban Fuentes, and Marie.

He made it, although he felt he was more dead than alive. The two girls hovered over him, plying him with hot coffee and insisting that he try to eat something. His eyes were closing when they supported him up the stairs to his room. He flung himself across the bed and was instantly asleep.

Two days later Walt Slade sat in the sheriff's office and talked with Tobe Medford.

"Everything's working out fine," the sheriff said. "The gents affiliated with the Land Committee are out on bail, awaiting trial. I've rounded up some of their hired gun-slingers and have them locked up along with the *bandidos*, and the rest are on the run. I figure the ones in the calaboose will do a bit of testifying when the matter comes to court. Folks on this side and the other side of the river are friendly again. The railroad's coming along. The syndicate has formally announced the irrigation project. We're locating the folks who were cheated out of their land and telling them to get the heck back here and make ready for the spring planting. The town's advancing money to tide them over till their crops grow. I think you were loco to turn down the reward they voted you, but I reckon you know your business. Anyhow, it looks like you set things right, per usual."

"With considerable help from you and the boys and, incidentally, Ralpho Flores," Slade replied.

"Suppose you're riding now?"

Slade nodded. "Yes, the chances are Captain Jim will have another little chore lined up for me by the time I get back to the Post. He usually has. I'll spend the night at the Telo ranch, and then I'll ride north. Estaban and the girls are there. Estaban quit his job of range boss for old Don Manuel and will handle the spread. He plans to do a lot of planting. So I'll be seeing you before long, I hope."

"Yep, I expect you will," agreed the sheriff. "Ain't far from the Telo ranch to here."

Slade spent two nights at the Telo ranch. On the morning of the second day, Marie stood beside his stirrup as he prepared to ride north to where duty called and new adventure waited.

"You'll be back," she stated softly, rather than asked.

And Walt Slade answered, "Yes."

THE END